DEATH AT YOUR BACK

The little girl was in the stable doorway. She had wide brown eyes and her face was streaked with dirt and grime.

Fargo smiled and lowered the Colt so as not to scare her.

"Run," the girl said.

Chuckling, Fargo replied, "Yes, you sure can. You're faster than a jackrabbit. I couldn't catch you if I tried."

"No. You, mister. You should run."

"Me?" Fargo said, unsure what she was getting at.

"He will come, and he'll be mad. He doesn't like anyone in here. This is his place."

"Who?" Fargo asked, hoping it was an adult, someone who could fill him in on what was going on.

"The bad man."

"Why do you say he's bad?"

"He has to be. He killed four people." She gazed past him and her eyes grew wide as saucers.

At the same instant, the hay rustled. Fargo turned and started to bring up the Colt but he was too slow. . . .

THE
TRAILSMAN
#264

SNAKE
RIVER RUINS

by

Jon Sharpe

A SIGNET BOOK

SIGNET
Published by New American Library, a division of
Penguin Group (USA) Inc., 375 Hudson Street,
New York, New York 10014, U.S.A.
Penguin Books Ltd, 80 Strand,
London WC2R 0RL, England
Penguin Books Australia Ltd, 250 Camberwell Road,
Camberwell, Victoria 3124, Australia
Penguin Books Canada Ltd, 10 Alcorn Avenue,
Toronto, Ontario, Canada M4V 3B2
Penguin Books (N.Z.) Ltd, Cnr Rosedale and Airborne Roads,
Albany, Auckland 1310, New Zealand

Penguin Books Ltd, Registered Offices:
80 Strand, London WC2R 0RL, England

First published by Signet, an imprint of New American Library,
a division of Penguin Group (USA) Inc.

First Printing, October 2003
10 9 8 7 6 5 4 3 2 1

The first chapter of this book previously appeared in *Arkansas Assault,*
the two hundred sixty-third volume in this series.

PUBLISHER'S NOTE
This is a work of fiction. Names, characters, places, and incidents either are
the product of the author's imagination or are used fictitiously, and any resem-
blance to actual persons, living or dead, business establishments, events, or
locales is entirely coincidental.

The Trailsman

Beginnings . . . they bend the tree and they mark the man. Skye Fargo was born when he was eighteen. Terror was his midwife, vengeance his first cry. Killing spawned Skye Fargo, ruthless, cold-blooded murder. Out of the acrid smoke of gunpowder still hanging in the air, he rose, cried out a promise never forgotten.

The Trailsman they began to call him all across the West: searcher, scout, hunter, the man who could see where others only looked, his skills for hire but not his soul, the man who lived each day to the fullest, yet trailed each tomorrow. Skye Fargo, the Trailsman, the seeker who could take the wildness of a land and the wanting of a woman and make them his own.

Washington Territory, early 1861—
Where the promise of a new life
reaped horrible death.

1

The big man in buckskins did not know what to make of it. Rising in the stirrups, he studied the stretch of dirt road ahead. His piercing lake-blue eyes flicked from the wagon that sat in the middle of the road to the woodland on either side. Something wasn't right.

Skye Fargo slid his right hand to the Colt on his hip. He had survived as long as he had by always heeding his instincts and they were telling him he must proceed with caution. He clucked to the Ovaro and rode on at a slow walk, alert for anything out of the ordinary. All seemed as it should be except that he didn't hear any birds. Usually, where there were a lot of trees, there would be sparrows and robins and jays and ravens, yet the woods were deathly still.

The wagon was a one-horse farm wagon, common on the frontier, with a bed nine feet long, a high seat at the front, and large wooden hubs. What it didn't have was the farmer who owned it or a horse to pull it. Apparently, it had been abandoned. Which begged the question: Why?

Dismounting, Fargo checked the wheels and the springs and the tongue. They were in working order. Nothing was broken. It made no sense for the owner to have left the wagon sitting there. Even stranger, part of the harness was still attached. Squatting, Fargo examined it. The harness had been cut.

The tracks were plain enough for a seasoned tracker to read, and Fargo was one of the best. They told him

1

the farmer had jumped down from the seat, cut the horse loose, climbed onto it, and galloped off to the west. All of which spelled trouble. The farmer had needed to get out of there in a hurry or he would have never cut expensive harness. Someone, or something, had spooked him.

Fargo made a circuit of the wagon. His first guess was hostiles, although to his knowledge, none of the local tribes were acting up. His second guess was outlaws but that seemed even less likely. The Palouse River country of southeastern Washington Territory held little to attract the lawless breed. He found no other recent prints, nothing that would explain the mystery.

Baffled, Fargo forked leather and lifted his reins. A crudely painted sign five miles back had pointed him in the direction of a settlement called Carn, where he intended to buy coffee and sugar and a few other items he was running low on, and push on.

The region consisted of gently rolling hills broken by isolated buttes and scattered tracts of woodland. It was sparsely populated but Fargo imagined that would change in a few years as word of its rich soil spread. He would be sorry to see that happen. There were already too many people flocking west.

Fargo couldn't explain it, but suddenly he felt overrun by uneasiness. Having learned to trust his instincts, he twisted in the saddle but saw nothing to account for it. His hand on his Colt, he gigged the pinto stallion north. He was almost clear of the trees when movement in the brush caused him to rein up again. He caught a flash of grayish-brown. Something had been there but now it was gone. After a minute he trotted into the open.

The heat hit him like a physical force. It was an exceptionally hot summer, with daytime temperatures well above one hundred degrees and nighttime temperatures dipping only to the mid-eighties. Drought had the land in a stranglehold. Streams that normally ran year-round had dried up. Springs that had always been reliable were bone dry. Were it not for the Palouse River to the north and the Snake River to the south, there wouldn't be a drop of water to be had anywhere.

Fargo's canteen was almost empty, yet another reason to visit Carn. The settlement was bound to have water. Or so he hoped. It wasn't uncommon for droughts as severe as this one to wither whole communities and leave ghost towns in their wake.

The vegetation was in dire need of rain. All the grass was brown and brittle. The trees drooped like ranks of old men about to keel into their graves, their branches bent, their leaves the same color as the baked earth.

Pulling his hat brim low against the harsh glare of the burning sun, Fargo mopped at his forehead with the sleeve of his buckskin shirt. He was caked with sweat. His mouth was dry, his throat parched, but he resisted the temptation to take a sip from his canteen. He could wait until he reached Carn.

The settlement was new. Fargo knew nothing about it but imagined it was no different from countless others he had come across in his travels. The road wound over a low hill and when he came to the crest he spotted a large animal lying on its side west of the road.

As Fargo approached, a swarm of flies rose thick into the air. The stench was awful. He had found a dead cow. Staying well away, he circled it. The cause of death wasn't readily obvious. It might have died of thirst. It might have been killed by a mountain lion or a bear. The eyes and throat were gone. So was the soft underbelly and its hindquarters. Coyote prints placed the blame for the missing parts on scavengers.

Fargo continued north. One dead cow in and of itself was not unusual. But in another mile he came on a second, and soon after, a third. Both were in the same state of decomposition. He wondered if maybe an outbreak of disease was to blame.

Carn lay nestled in a broad valley at the base of the

hills. From a slope half a mile away, Fargo counted two dozen buildings. Most flanked the town's lone street. Holding to a walk, he soon came to a house that stood off by itself. A stone fence bordered a neatly trimmed yard. Once, a flower bed had flourished, but now the flowers were dead, their petals shriveled like burnt leaves.

Fargo was almost past the fence when he spotted a dead dog. It lay on its side, its tongue jutting from its mouth, its eyes glazed. The cause of death was hard to tell. There wasn't a mark on it. The mouth crawled with flies. Plainly, it had been dead for several days.

Puzzled as to why its owner hadn't buried it, Fargo glanced at the house. A rocking chair lay overturned on the porch, and the front door hung open. He drew rein and cupped a hand to his mouth. "Anyone home?"

No one answered.

Dismounting, Fargo walked to the gate. It was ajar wide enough for him to step on through, and then along a cobblestone walk to the porch. "Is anyone here?" Silence mocked him. He knocked but no one came to the door. Poking his head inside, he saw a coat stand on the hall floor. On the wall beside it was a smear of blood.

Palming his Colt, Fargo entered. The parlor was a shambles. Most of the furniture had been thrown violently about, and a chair cushion had been torn apart. He checked all the downstairs rooms but none of the others had been disturbed. As he climbed the stairs a familiar stench wreathed him, and he untied his red bandanna from around his neck and retied it over his nose and mouth.

He thought he would find another dead dog or maybe a cat. The first two bedrooms were empty but the door to the third was closed. Pushing it open, he nearly gagged at the odor. On the bed lay the source, an elderly man, fully clothed, a peaceful smile on his wrinkled face. The top of his head had been blown off. Beside him lay a shotgun.

Fargo closed the door and went outside. He sucked in long breaths to clear his lungs, and paused at the gate. He was unsure what to make of it all. Why had the old man been left there like that? Hadn't anyone noticed something was amiss?

The Ovaro had its ears pricked and was staring toward the settlement a hundred yards away. Fargo looked but saw no one. Possibly the heat had driven them indoors. But that did not explain the absence of horses at the hitch rails, nor the absence of all sound.

"I don't like this," Fargo said to the pinto as he stepped into the stirrups. Halfway between the house and the outskirts lay a rotting cat. Farther on, next to a dry horse trough, was another dead dog. "What the hell is going on?"

Fargo rode down the center of the street searching for inhabitants. No one appeared in any of the doorways or windows. Nor did he hear a single human voice. It was as if all the people had up and vanished.

Fargo had been in ghost towns before. Many a boomtown had gone bust, forcing the people to go elsewhere to earn a livelihood. But this was different. He had a feeling of foreboding, a sense that something was gravely wrong and he should light a shuck while he still could.

At the hitch rail in front of the general store, Fargo reined in. He slid down, shucked his Henry rifle from the saddle scabbard, levered a round into the chamber, and stepped onto the plank boardwalk. "Anyone here?" he called out. Again silence taunted him. He tried the latch and the door swung in on well-oiled hinges. The interior was stifling hot.

His spurs jangling, Fargo moved down the center aisle. The store was clean and tidy. The shelves were fully stocked with everything from dry goods and tools to bolts of cloth for making dresses. A birdcage hung from a low beam but the cage was empty, its tiny door open. He came to the counter and ran a finger across it. There was no dust. Which meant that whoever owned it had not been gone for long.

Coffee, tea and sugar were on a shelf behind the counter. Fargo was about to help himself when he decided to check the rest of the town. There might be a perfectly logical explanation for the missing settlers. Maybe they were having a town meeting. Or maybe they were attending a funeral. He went back outside.

The Ovaro's head was drooping, its eyes half-closed. Fargo wished there were some shade handy but he did not intend to stay long. He peered into building after building but they were all the same. At the end of the street stood the stable, its double doors wide open. Across from it was a freshly painted church with a tall steeple. Just as he set eyes on it, the bell in the belfry clanged.

Fargo smiled to himself. So that was where they were. Rather than interrupt their services, he crossed to the saloon and pushed on the bat-wing doors. As saloons went it had little to recommend it. A few tables, a dozen bottles of liquor, and a painting above the bar of a plump woman in a full-length dress. In a corner sat a piano. No one was there, which was mildly surprising. Most towns, no matter how small, had their share of folks who wouldn't set foot in God's house if they were paid to. And the saloon was where they spent most of their time.

Shrugging, Fargo walked behind the bar and helped himself to a bottle of coffin varnish. It wasn't the best but it washed the dust from his throat and put a knot of warmth in his stomach. Not that he needed to be any warmer. The windows were shut and it had to be one hundred and ten degrees in there, if not more.

Selecting a table, Fargo sat with his back to a wall and filled a glass. He drank slowly, hoping the church service or whatever it was would end soon and he could get on with his business and get out of there. But after twenty minutes he grew impatient and walked into the street.

Not a sign of life was to be seen. No dogs, no cats, no pigs wandering aimlessly or chickens scratching in the dust. He unwound the Ovaro's reins from the hitch rail and made for the stable. The trough in front was bone dry. He walked the stallion inside and received another surprise. The stalls were empty. Every last one. But if the horses weren't there, where were they?

Even with the doors open the stable was a furnace. Fargo led the Ovaro back out and over to a trough near the church. It, too, was dry. But there had to be water somewhere.

The church bell clanged again.

Fargo decided enough was enough. He strode up to the door and opened it. A gust of hot air fanned his face as he removed his hat and entered. It took a few seconds for his eyes to adjust, and when he did, he couldn't believe what he was seeing. No one was there. The church was as deserted as the rest of the town.

The bell clanged, and Fargo hurried past the pews to a small door to the belfry. He opened it, and wished he hadn't. An abominable reek filled his nose before he could think to hold his breath. His stomach churned, spewing bitter bile into his throat. Covering his mouth with his hand, he backed out. The reek followed, clinging like invisible mist.

The image of what Fargo had seen was seared into his brain; the bell far overhead, a rope suspended from it, and suspended from the rope, the parson. A noose had dug deep into the minister's neck and his face was swollen and discolored. From the grisly look of things, he had been hanging there a couple of days, if not longer.

Anxious for a breath of untainted air, Fargo hurried out and leaned on the rail. To the growing mysteries was added another; had the parson been hanged, or had he hanged himself? Regardless of which it was, why had the good people of Carn left the man there to rot? The more Fargo found, the less sense it made.

"Where is everyone?" Fargo shouted, and when he received no reply, he smacked the rail in frustration.

The Ovaro was staring down the street again, its ears pricked as before. Fargo stepped past it but saw

nothing. "Damn it. There has to be someone around."
Pointing the Henry at the ground, he banged off a
shot. The slug kicked up dirt, but that was all it did.
No one appeared. No doors or windows were flung
open. No shouts were raised.

That was when the full grim truth hit him; Fargo
realized he must be the only living person in Carn.
Everyone else was either gone—or dead. But why?
And where to? An epidemic wasn't to blame. Not
unless it was an illness that made people hang themselves or put a gun to their own heads.

Fargo had a sudden urge to get out of there. To
put as many miles as he could between himself and
Carn. He shoved the Henry into its scabbard, climbed
on the pinto, and reined south. He had no personal
stake in whatever was going on here. When he
reached Fort Bridger he would report what he had
found. Let the army deal with it.

The *clomp* of the stallion's heavy hooves seemed
unnaturally loud. Fargo came to the general store, and
stopped. He had come this far, he might as well get
what he came for. Quickly, he swung down. "I'll be
right back." He took a step, then whirled.

Across the street a door had slammed.

Every nerve taut, Fargo listened. He thought he
heard footsteps but he couldn't be sure. He scanned
every window, every doorway. If someone was there,
why hadn't they shown themselves?

More eager than ever to light a shuck, Fargo piled
coffee, sugar, matches and ammunition on the counter.
He left enough money to cover the cost and scooped
everything into his arms. Another minute and it was
all in his saddlebags and he was on his way. *Good
riddance,* he thought.

Fargo was not going to look back, but as he passed
the last building he did. And involuntarily stiffened.
A face was watching him from a second floor window.
It was a young girl, as pale as snow, stringy bangs
hanging to her eyebrows. "I'll be damned!" he

blurted, and smiled and waved. The girl melted into the murk behind her.

Fargo never hesitated. In a twinkling he was off the Ovaro. The door was locked but he did not let that stop him. Lowering his shoulder, he stepped back, then slammed into it hard enough to splinter the wood and tear it off a hinge. He was in a feed and grain store. Farm implements were everywhere.

To Fargo's left were stairs. He took them three at a bound. At the top he paused to get his bearings. The window the child had been at was in a room on the right. "Little girl?" He barreled on in. It was a storeroom for sacks of seed piled almost to the ceiling. He had to thread through them to reach the window. The room had not been dusted in ages, and there in the dust under the window were small footprints. He hadn't been seeing things.

"Girl, where are you? I won't hurt you." Fargo checked the storeroom and had just stepped into the hall when a crash downstairs brought him to the stairs in a rush. A shadow flitted across the front window. He raced down and on out into the glare of the sun. Blinking, he looked both ways, but the girl, if indeed she had been responsible, was gone.

Fargo gazed south. In half an hour he could reach the main trail. By the end of the day he could be halfway to the border. Instead, he went into the middle of the street and tried again. "Girl? Where are you?" He didn't expect her to answer and she didn't disappoint him.

Suddenly Fargo heard a soft sound behind him. Thinking it must be her, he smiled and turned, saying, "I meant what I said about not hurting you. All I want—" His voice died in his throat.

It wasn't the girl. It was a cat. A big gray tabby, the kind found in every town in the country. It was larger than most, almost the size of a bobcat, but thin as a rail. Crouched low, it growled and twitched its tail.

"Go chase mice, you idiot," Fargo declared, and clapped his hands, thinking to drive it off. But the cat hissed and stalked toward him. He did not want to hurt it if he could help it; maybe it belonged to the little girl. But when the tabby bared its teeth and coiled to spring, Fargo dropped his hand to his Colt. "Get out of here!" he tried one more time.

Hissing, the cat leaped.

Fargo drew and shot it in midair. The slug caught the feline in the forehead, and it didn't move after it fell. Nudging it with the tip of his boot, he commented, "Damned peculiar."

As was his habit, Fargo immediately replaced the spent cartridge. It gave him time to think. He couldn't just ride off and leave the little girl. But neither did he like the notion of spending the rest of the afternoon scouring Carn from bottom to top. Maybe there was another way, a better way.

Leading the Ovaro, Fargo returned to the general store. A jar near the cracker barrel contained the bait he needed. He took it with him to the saloon, tied the pinto to the rail, then placed the jar below the batwing doors, where he could see it from inside.

Fargo wasn't musically inclined. He had pounded on a few ivories for the fun of it when he was drunk enough not to care, but that was it. Taking a seat at the piano, he did his best to imitate a piano player. He was awful but that was all right because he wasn't trying to impress anyone. The important thing was that the tinny notes would carry from one end of Carn to the other and the girl was bound to hear.

Fargo kept one eye on the jar of hard candy. He played until his fingers were sore but the jar went untouched. Just when he figured it was more than likely his plunking had scared her off rather than made her curious, tiny hands seized the jar and snatched it away.

He was up off the bench and to the door in three long strides but it wasn't fast enough. He caught a glimpse of sandy hair and skinny legs as the girl darted into the next doorway down. The door slammed, and by the time he reached it she had thrown the bolt. A sign announced it was the barbershop. He raised his boot to kick the door in, then thought better of the idea. It would only frighten her more.

Darting to the window, Fargo saw the girl at the rear of the shop, opening the back door. He ran around the side and flew to the corner. She was just going around the opposite one. He gave chase.

The girl couldn't be more than ten or twelve, but damn, she was fast. When Fargo reached the other side she was already to the street. His body protesting the exertion, he ran flat out. He was sweating worse than ever and his lungs were laboring twice as hard as they should but it couldn't be helped.

The girl had gone to the right, so without breaking stride, Fargo did, too. He went twenty feet and drew up short in consternation. She had disappeared again. "Damn!" Leaning against a wall to catch his breath, he listened for her footsteps, or any other sound. There were none. She was clever as a fox, he would say that for her.

Hardly had Fargo entertained the thought than he glanced up the street and saw an animal in the doorway of the stable, staring at him. It was a red fox. He closed his eyes and opened them again and the fox was still there, so it must be real. But foxes came out at night, not during the day, and always fought shy of human habitation.

Fargo stepped to the end of the boardwalk. He figured the fox would run off but it stood there watching him with an intensity that was unsettling. He moved into the street to see it better and the thing finally did what foxes were supposed do; it spun and loped off around the stable.

Shaking his head, Fargo walked to the Ovaro. Since he couldn't bring himself to ride off and leave the girl, he might as well get the stallion in out of the sun. He took it to the stable, palming his Colt as he neared the double doors. He wasn't taking any chances. A search turned up no other wildlife or feral cats, so he stripped off the bridle, saddle and saddle blanket, and placed the pinto in a stall. The feed bins were filled to overflowing. He gave the stallion as much grain as he thought it should have, closed the stall, and was bending to grab his Henry and his saddlebags when something rustled in the hayloft above.

His skin crawling, Fargo backed up several steps and drew his Colt. "Is someone up there?"

The rustling was repeated.

To his left a ladder was propped against the loft. Fargo started up, stopping several times to listen. When he was high enough, he peered over the edge but all he saw were mounds of hay. He told himself he must have heard a mouse or a rat. He should forget about it and go look for the girl but his infernal curiosity would not be denied.

Climbing the rest of the way, Fargo straightened. The heat was nearly unbearable. He sidled to one side but there was nothing to account for the rustling. He heard the Ovaro nicker, and glancing down, he froze.

The little girl was in the stable doorway. She was sucking on a piece of hard candy, the jar cradled in her arm. She had wide brown eyes and her face was streaked with dirt and grime. Her dress was torn and filthy, her shoes caked with dust.

Fargo smiled and lowered the Colt so as not to scare her. "Like sweets, do you? I figured you might. Most your age do."

"Run," the girl said.

Chuckling, Fargo replied, "Yes, you sure can. You're faster than a jackrabbit. I couldn't catch you if I tried."

"No. You, mister. You should run."

"Me?" Fargo said, unsure what she was getting at. How could he run when he was up in the loft?

The girl stopped sucking. "He will come, and he'll be mad. He doesn't like anyone in here. This is his place."

"Who?" Fargo asked, hoping it was an adult, someone who could fill him in on what was going on.

"The bad man."

"Why do you say he's bad?" Fargo had never been a parent but he knew how kids her age had a knack for exaggeration.

"He has to be. He's killed four people." She gazed past him and her eyes grew as wide as saucers.

At the same instant, the hay rustled again. Fargo turned and started to bring up the Colt but he was too slow. A scarecrow was lunging out of the shadows at him. He only had a fraction of a second to register a craggy face twisted in hate and eyes in which madness gleamed. Too late, he saw the pitchfork in the scarecrow's right hand. Glistening tines speared at his chest.

Without thinking, Fargo threw himself backward, but in doing so, he pitched headlong off the hayloft.

2

The blur of the fall ended in the jolt of impact. As he plummeted, Skye Fargo twisted to try to land on his side and in that he was successful. His right shoulder and arm bore the brunt. The pain wasn't that bad. He had felt worse. But his arm went completely numb and the Colt went skittering off into a stall.

Fargo glanced at the hayloft. He half thought the crazed scarecrow might hurl the pitchfork. But no, his attacker was coming down the ladder after him.

"Won't get me! Won't get me!" the man maniacally gibbered over and over. He had on bib overalls and a cotton shirt, neither of which had been washed in ages.

Propping his left hand under him, Fargo heaved to his feet. He had to find the Colt before the lunatic reached him. But he had barely turned toward the stall when the man with the pitchfork jumped down and came at him brandishing it like a Cheyenne war lance.

"Gonna kill you! Gonna kill you dead!"

Fargo skipped aside and the tines missed by a whisker. He tried to grab the handle with his right hand but his right arm wouldn't move. Before he could try with his left, the man stabbed at his face. Fargo ducked, then had to weave and dance as the man thrust again and again and again.

The scarecrow cackled. "Not here you won't! I'm too smart! It won't get me like it got the others! You hear? You hear? Stand still, damn your hide, and let me finish it!" He cackled and lunged.

Fargo focused on the pitchfork and only the pitchfork. With all his spinning and twisting, he was now ten feet from the stall the Colt had slid into. And the lunatic was between him and the stall. When the man paused again, winded, Fargo said, "Why in hell are you trying to kill me?"

"Better to nip it in the bud," the man said, and tittered. "You don't kill a rattler by choppin' off its tail." He had the pitchfork close to his waist, the tines pointed at Fargo. "How do you think I've lasted this long? Because I never give them the benefit of the doubt."

"Mister, I don't know what you're talking about," Fargo admitted. "What happened to this town? Where is everyone?"

"As if you don't know." The man crouched. "You won't get away. You can't get past me and soon I'll have you backed into a corner. Then it will all be over but the howlin'."

Fargo was flexing and unflexing his right hand, hoping to regain use of his arm. The pitchfork sheared at his neck and he sprang out of the way. More thrusts drove him further back. When the scarecrow stopped, he glanced over his shoulder and saw he only had a few feet to go and he would be out of room.

"Your time is about up." The man was breathing heavily. "You're quicker than most or I'd have done you in by now. When it's over I'll feed you to them. They like that. I think that's why they let me be."

"Who does?" Fargo's right arm was tingling and he could bend his elbow but not far enough. He attempted to stall. "At least tell me why you want to kill me. Is that too much to ask?"

"You must think I'm as loco as you are."

"Me?" Any other time, the irony of being called crazy by a madman would be amusing. Now all it did was make Fargo mad. "This is your last chance. Put that thing down and let's talk."

"Sure. Whatever you want." The scarecrow grinned and made as if to drop the pitchfork to the ground. Instead, more fiercely than ever, he renewed his assault. "Die! Die!"

Fargo saved his groin by twisting sharply to one side. He wrapped his left hand around the handle and tried to hold on but the scarecrow was a lot stronger than he looked, and the pitchfork was torn from his grasp.

"That won't do, neighbor! That won't do at all!"

Another step and Fargo's back made contact with the wall. It was the moment the lunatic had been waiting for. Raising the pitchfork shoulder high, he screeched with demented glee and stabbed at Fargo's chest. Fargo wrenched his body to the left but one of the tines pierced his shirt and he felt cold steel scrape his ribs.

The man drew back to try again. "I've got you now!"

"Like hell you do." Fargo kicked him in the knee. Screeching, the lunatic doubled over, putting his grizzled face right where Fargo wanted it. He snap-kicked his boot into the other man's jaw, sending him onto his back where he lay thrashing like an upended turtle. He held onto the pitchfork, though, and when Fargo moved in close, he speared it at Fargo's stomach.

A bound carried Fargo out of reach. Whirling, he ran to the stall where the Colt should be but didn't see it. Either it was in the shadows or covered by straw. Dropping onto his hands and knees, he groped about. It had to be there.

"Lookin' for water, are you?" The man blocked the end of the stall, his pitchfork poised to strike. "You won't find any here. I took the handle and hid it. I'll be damned if I'll share. I dug it and it's mine!" He closed for the kill.

Fargo found the Colt. And he could use his right arm again. He fired as the tines swept at his face, he fired as the lunatic stumbled back, he fired as the man crumpled. His ears ringing, he slowly rose.

Slumped against the stall, the man looked down at

16

the holes in his scrawny chest. "No fair!" he bleated. "You've gone and shot me! What kind of a thing is that to do to someone tryin' to do you a favor?"

"Favor, hell. You wanted to skewer me, you bastard." Fargo felt no sympathy whatsoever. "You brought this on yourself."

"Not me! The wind brought it. The others said I was out of my mind but I knew!" His voice grew weaker with each word. "It was the wind, you hear me? A wind straight from hell. The breath of the devil, it was, and now look." The man did a strange thing then. He smiled as friendly as could be, said, "I forgive you, sonny, for being so stupid." And he died.

Fargo stepped over the body and on past the Ovaro. His saddlebags were lying where he had left them. He started to reload, then glanced down again. The Henry was gone. It had been lying beside his saddlebags but now it wasn't there. He turned to the doorway. The girl wasn't there, either. While he was fighting for his life she had slipped in and stolen it. He dashed out into the street but she was long gone. She could be anywhere.

Sliding the Colt into its holster, Fargo bent his steps to the general store. He didn't care to be without a rifle and that was the likeliest place to find one since Carn didn't have a gun shop. He remembered seeing a gun cabinet when he was in there but he hadn't looked inside.

Fargo left the front door open so he could hear if someone came down the street. He had to pass the canned goods to reach the gun cabinet, and he stopped. As thirsty as he was, he should have thought of this sooner. He read each of the labels. On the top shelf he found what he was he was looking for; canned peaches. Taking one down, he set it on the counter. To open it he used a large butcher knife.

His throat was parched. He only had the top half off when he tipped the can to his mouth and let the sweet syrup slowly trickle down his throat. The taste was delicious, the relief it brought immense. He savored every drop.

Removing the top, Fargo forked out the peach halves and wolfed them as if he hadn't eaten in a month. When he was done he ambled to the gun cabinet. It was locked but an axe solved that problem. The only gun it contained was a shotgun for which there was no ammunition. Someone had taken all the rifles.

Fargo didn't return to the stable empty-handed, though. He took the other two cans of peaches, a "canned cow," as cowboys called canned milk, several cans of Van Camp's beans, cheese, raisins and crackers. He deposited them with his saddlebags and went out again.

The sun was well past its zenith. Fargo estimated he had five to six hours of daylight left. Plenty of time to do what needed to be done. Now that he had temporarily slaked his own thirst, he intended to do the same for the Ovaro. There must be water nearby. The lunatic could not have survived for long in the intense heat without it.

Fargo walked around to the back of the stable. The corral was empty. Parked next to it was a buckboard. He turned to go, then noticed footprints and scrape marks near the buckboard's front wheel. It looked to him as if someone had gotten down on their hands and knees and crawled underneath.

Drawing the Colt, Fargo squatted. With all that had happened, he didn't think anything could surprise him. He was wrong. Under the buckboard was a pump. Someone, the lunatic, no doubt, had parked the buckboard over it. But why? To hide it? Everyone in Carn must know it was there.

Wrapping both arms around the tongue, Fargo dug in his boot heels and pulled. It took some doing to get the wheels rolling. The pump, however, wouldn't work. The handle was gone.

Fargo remembered the scarecrow saying he had hid it. The logical place to start looking was the hayloft. He took the pitchfork with him and spent a quarter of an hour poking through the hay. He was about to call it quits when he thrust the fork into a pile in a corner and metal rang on metal. Sweeping the hay aside, he grinned. "I'm not as stupid as you thought, old man."

To reattach the handle required a linchpin, bolt and nut, but fortunately the lunatic had left them lying next to the pump, along with a tool tray. Fargo also took a bucket from a peg on the wall.

Once the job was done, Fargo pumped slowly, then with increasing vigor when no water came out. He stuck a finger up the spout but the spout was dry. Undaunted, he continued to pump until his arms were tired. He let go to stretch and relieve a cramp, and heard a gurgling sound. The next moment, a wet ribbon trickled into the bucket. He resumed pumping, harder than before, but pump as he might, the flow never changed. He kept at it until the bucket was almost full. By then his shoulders were throbbing and his arms were leaden.

Fargo turned to go. He was so excited about the water, he hadn't been paying much attention to his surroundings.

A thin man about thirty years of age was a stone's throw away, staring at him with the most peculiar expression.

"I didn't hear you come up," Fargo said. "Care for some water?" He held the bucket out to show how much he had.

The man's reaction was bewildering. Recoiling as if he had been slapped, he clutched at his throat, threw back his head, and shrieked. Then, in defiance of all reason, he whirled and sprinted off across the grassland toward the brown hills.

"What the hell?" Fargo was beginning to think everyone in Carn had gone stark, raving nuts. He watched until the man was almost to the trees, then he carried the bucket into the stable and over to the Ovaro's stall. He was lifting it for the stallion to drink when the distinct rasp of a gun hammer being cocked warned him he had more company.

The girl was back, and she had brought someone else, an attractive woman with the same sandy hair and the same brown eyes and oval chin. She wore a homespun dress that had seen better days and her face was haggard but determined. She also had his Henry trained on his chest. "We'll take that water, if you don't mind, mister. And even if you do, I'm afraid."

"You're her mother, I take it?"

"Gwendolyn is one of mine, yes," the woman confirmed. "I'm Devona Carroway. Most hereabouts call me Devy. We have a farm southeast of here. She strayed off and I came looking. I was afraid they'd gotten her."

"Who had?"

"Set the bucket down and step back. I don't want to shoot you but I will if I have to. Water is precious in these parts since the drought struck."

Fargo did as she wanted. "I don't suppose you would be willing to share? Half for you and your girl, half for my horse?"

"People count for more than critters in my book." Devy came toward him, her finger around the trigger. She had a full bosom, wide hips, and long legs, the kind a man could lose himself in. "I'm sorry your horse has to go without, but that's just how things are."

"My horse has as much right to drink as you do," Fargo said. He was trying to make her understand his position but she didn't want to hear it.

"Keep quiet. I don't like what I'm doing any better than you do. But then, I've had to do a lot of things I never thought I would since this whole nightmare began." Devy saw the lunatic's legs poking out of the stall, and stopped. "Is that Malachi? Gwen told me he came after you with that pitchfork of his."

"Was that his name?" Fargo didn't take his eyes off the Henry. The barrel had dipped a few inches.

"Malachi Strum. He owned the stable. The drought hit him hard. He had six fine horses once. But he couldn't raise enough water from his well to keep them alive. When the killing started he barred the doors. And he'd shoot anyone who came near his pump." Sadness etched Devy's features. "He must have run out of ammunition long ago, same as me."

"The doors weren't barred when I rode in," Fargo said to keep her talking. The Henry had dipped another half inch. A little more, and the muzzle would be pointed at the ground.

"He had to forage to stay alive, same as the rest of us. You must have shown up when he was about to go out." Devy stepped to the bucket.

Fargo tensed his legs. "I saw a fox standing about where your daughter is. Strange, it coming in close like that."

"I'm not surprised. Wild critters need to eat too, and there isn't much left anywhere. Or maybe it was one of them, in which case you were lucky it didn't try to bite you."

"Them?" Fargo repeated, watching her bend and grip the bucket's handle. He waited until she was unfurling, with her one hand burdened and her body off-balance, and leaped. He heard the daughter scream a warning. The mother whipped the Henry around but she was burdened by the heavy bucket. Seizing the barrel, Fargo tore the rifle from her grasp and raised a hand to slap her.

"Don't you dare!" Gwen darted between them and wrapped her arms around her mother's leg. "If you hurt my ma, I'll hurt you!"

Fargo lowered his arm, his anger fading. "Step over there," he commanded, indicating the ladder. When they complied, he leaned the Henry against the stall. "I can't say I think much of the hospitality around here," he commented as he lifted the bucket to the Ovaro.

"You just don't know," Devy said. Her shoulders had slumped and her lower lip was quivering. "You just don't know what it's been like."

"I've lived through a few droughts," Fargo said. In Texas once he'd seen entire herds wiped out. In Kansas he'd seen the wheat and corn crops shriveled to nothing. Families lost virtually everything they owned.

"Never like this."

The Ovaro had its nose in the bucket and was drinking as if it could not get enough. Fargo kept one eye on the street to avoid having more nasty surprises sprung on him. "How many people are left?"

"I can't rightly say. Carn is a farming community. It had a population of fifty-three, including the folks in the outlying farms. Those who didn't die of thirst were either eaten by the hellhounds or bitten."

"Hellhounds?"

Devy absently ran her fingers through her daughter's hair. "That's what most everyone calls them. Flannery thought we should call them hellbreeds, since they're half and half. Not that it makes a difference. As God is my witness, they are the vilest abominations to ever roam the earth."

Gwen trembled and hugged her mother tighter. "Don't talk about them, ma. It scares me."

Devy was staring at Fargo. "Surely you saw some on your way in?"

"Lady, I don't have any damn idea what you're talking about. All I saw were dead cows until I reached town."

"You were lucky. If they had caught you in the open, they would chase your horse into the ground and devour the both of you." Now it was the mother who trembled. "That's what they did to my husband six months ago."

"The dry spell has lasted that long?"

Devy shook her head. "The hellhounds were here long before the drought started. There's no connection between the two except that the drought made it more difficult for them to find wild things to kill so they started in on humans."

Fargo set the bucket down, cradled the Henry in the crook of his left elbow, and motioned. "Why don't you make yourselves comfortable? I'd like to hear more. If you promise to behave, you can have a can of peaches." He rolled one toward the daughter and gave the butcher knife to the mother.

Gwen snatched up the can and clasped it to her as if it were the greatest treasure in the world. "Look, ma! Won't it be grand? We haven't had any in a coon's age!"

"They were on a shelf at the general store," Fargo said.

"We haven't been in Carn in weeks. We were too afraid to leave our house." Devy sat with her knees tucked under her and jabbed the knife into the top of the can. "We wouldn't be here now except my youngest snuck off and I had to come after her." She gave Gwen a look of disapproval.

"I'm sorry, ma," Gwen said, "but we were out of food and almost out of water. With Billy sick—" She caught herself and covered her mouth.

"Who is Billy?" Fargo asked, puzzled by what she had done.

"My son," Devy answered. "He's fourteen." She hesitated. "I'm not sure what he came down with. But he was too weak to come with me to find Gwendolyn." She finished opening the can and slid it to her daughter. "Here. You first."

She plunged a hand in, scooped out a peach, and crammed it into her mouth. Syrup ran down over her chin and neck but she didn't care.

Taking a sip, Devy smacked her lips and smiled. "I'd forgotten how wonderful these taste." She passed the can to Gwen, then nodded at the bucket. "Is there any water left?"

"Help yourself." Fargo watched her closely until she sat back down. He didn't trust her yet, and wouldn't until she proved she wasn't about to shoot him or stab him in the back. "I'd like to hear more about the hellhounds."

"Where to begin?" Devy smoothed the front of her dress and fussed with her hair. "Carn sprang up about two and a half years ago. My husband and I arrived a couple of months later. Brian and I were on our

23

way to Oregon but we fell in love with this area. At the time it was green and lush. A Garden of Eden, we called it. We staked a claim to a hundred and sixty acres of bottomland and Brian put in crops."

Their domestic history was of no interest to Fargo but he was in no rush to leave so he could afford to be patient.

"Life was good. The Indians didn't bother us. There was plenty of game. Deer, rabbits, you name it. And coyotes. They would come in close to the house late at night and yip in the most marvelous symphony."

Fargo had heard a lot of coyotes in his travels but never any he would describe like that.

"Then some of Leon Hinkle's dogs ran off. Leon is from Georgia, and I'd swear he likes dogs better than he does people. He had twelve at one time but five of them disappeared and the next anyone knew, they were running with the coyotes."

"That happens from time to time."

"Do the dogs and coyotes mate? Because that's what these did. And the pups were nothing like the parents. They were halfbreeds. Part dog, part coyote, with the worst natures of both. They took to killing calves and foals and pets of all kinds." Devy stopped and fished a peach from the can. "Before another year was up, there were thirty to forty hellhounds running loose."

The number of pups a female coyote had varied, but Fargo knew of instances where a single female gave birth to up to nineteen at one time. It didn't happen often, but a few large litters like that would account for the forty hybrids. "Go on with your story."

"Some of the men set out to exterminate them. They laid traps, set snares, put poison in carcasses. A few were killed but nowhere near enough. So a town meeting was called. The mayor, Pete Dillard, suggested we pool our money and hire a professional hunter. But before anything could come of it, the drought set in and everyone had more important things to worry about than the hellhounds. Or so we thought."

"Something go wrong?" Fargo asked when she didn't go on.

"It's just that the next part is hard to talk about. You see, once a lot of the wildlife had died out because of the drought, the hellhounds started going after anything that lived, any hour of the day or night. Brian was coming home late from Carn one night. He had his rifle with him so he probably figured it was safe to do." Devy took a deep breath. "I was beside myself when ten o'clock rolled around and he hadn't shown. He was always home by nine to tuck the children in. Always."

"Did you go look for him?"

"Not at night, no. I wouldn't leave the children alone. I waited until dawn. I hadn't slept a wink all night but I saddled my mare and headed for Carn. About halfway I found his horse, or what was left of it. There was no trace of him so I came in and begged for help. Every last man came with me. Hinkle was in town and he had brought one of his hounds. It tracked Brian's scent to a gully." A haunted look crept into Devy's eyes. "There was less left of him than there had been of his horse. The hellhounds had stripped him to the bone. Everything except his face. It was hardly touched. I don't know why. But I'll never forget—" Tears were forming and she blinked them away.

"Oh, Ma," Gwen said in a small voice. "You never told me that."

"That's all I need to hear," Fargo said to spare the girl. He picked up the bucket. "I'll go refill this and be right back." Turning, he saw the red fox in the doorway at the same instant Devona Carroway whispered.

"Stop! Whatever you do, don't move!"

"It's just looking for food," Fargo said. Except when cornered, foxes were some of the most timid creatures alive.

25

"You don't understand," Devy whispered. "I didn't finish my story. You haven't heard the worst part yet."

Fargo looked at her. "What could be worse than the death of your husband, the hellhounds and the drought?"

"The rabies."

As she said it, the fox snarled and slunk toward them.

3

Rabies. Few words instilled as much fear on the frontier. All it took was a nip from an infected animal and the person bitten was doomed. There was no cure, no way to relieve the terrible suffering. Whoever came down with it died the worst imaginable death. As a precaution, rabid animals were always destroyed on sight. They had to be, for it didn't take much to turn a single case of rabies into a widespread epidemic.

It was no wonder Skye Fargo's skin crawled as the red fox crept toward them. It wasn't foaming at the mouth, which was a telltale sign, but not all animals did, especially during the early stages of the disease. It made them no less deadly. If the fox had rabies, and from its stiff-legged gait and the fact it was roaming around in broad daylight hinted it might, one bite would snuff out their lives.

Fargo still had the Henry in the crook of his elbow. A round was already in the chamber. All he had to do was drop the bucket, take quick aim, and fire. He released the handle and whipped the Henry up, but before he could squeeze the trigger, a red bolt of lightning streaked toward him. His first shot spun the fox around. His second slammed it to the dirt. His third and fourth weren't needed but he added them for good measure. "Rabies," he said softly, annoyed at not realizing it sooner. The cat that attacked him must have been rabid. The dead dog by the stone fence, too. And all the rest, besides.

"It's hard to say which has killed more," Devy said. "The rabies, the hellhounds or the heat." Her daughter was a statue, fearful eyes on the fox.

"How many people have come down with it?" Fargo asked to gauge just how severe the epidemic was.

Oddly, Devy hesitated. "Some. Old Man Tyler out at the edge of town was bit by his dog and blew his brains out rather than suffer. Our parson was bit by a cat and hung himself. Five or six others I can think of offhand."

Fargo replaced the spent cartridges. He usually left the chamber under the hammer empty as a precaution but with rabid animals running around, he loaded all six chambers. "We've got to get you and your daughter out of here."

"How? You have the only horse. And it can't carry all three of us very far in this heat." Devy rose, lifting Gwen with her. "Besides, there's my son to think of. I've been gone too long. He'll be frantic."

"We'll go together," Fargo proposed. "The two of you can ride and I'll walk."

"That's nice of you but we can manage on our own."

Fargo had known some pigheaded people but she beat them all. Alone and unarmed, they wouldn't stand a prayer if a rabid animal or the hellhounds found them. He pointed that out, adding, "It's no bother. We'll take the canned food along so your boy can have something to eat."

First Fargo had to get the fox out of the doorway. He used the pitchfork. The thing was heavier than it looked. He carried it past the door and around the corner and left it there, the pitchfork still imbedded in its body. As he turned, he gazed to the west and saw seven wolf-like shapes lope over a hill and make toward Carn.

Grabbing the door, Fargo pulled it shut and spun to warn Devy and her daughter. They weren't there. He ran back out and saw them hastening across the field to the east. "Wait!" he shouted, but they kept on walking. He overtook them in seconds and put a hand on Devy's shoulder only to have her shrug loose.

"Please. Don't try to stop us. We don't need your help."

"Answer one question for me," Fargo said, and pointed. "Are those some of the hellhounds you were telling me about?"

Strung out in a line, the largest in the lead, the pack had covered half the distance to town.

"Ma! It's them!" Gwen squealed. "They'll eat us like they did Pa!"

Incredibly, Devy Carroway glanced to the southeast as if she were seriously considering trying to outrun them.

"Think of your girl," Fargo said, and when she still stood there, he grabbed her wrist and headed back. For a moment she resisted. They only had a short distance to cover but the hellhounds were already dangerously close and moving with quicksilver speed.

Fargo pushed the Carroways inside and took hold of a door. "Grab the bar!" he shouted as he began to pull. He could see the leader of the pack clearly; a huge beast, twice the size of most dogs and coyotes, with a stocky body, a short snout and a mouth bristling with fangs. A second after he pulled the door shut, the leader struck it with a resounding crash. "Hurry," he urged.

"I'm trying." Devy had hold of the long bar but in her weakened condition it was too heavy for her to lift. "Help me."

Fargo couldn't. The hellhounds were slamming against both doors. His hands braced, he dug in his boot heels. He could hear the pack snarling and snapping in a frenzy.

Gwen screamed and ran under the hayloft.

The doors parted enough for a savage hairy face to poke through. Eyes ablaze with raw ferocity focused on Fargo as the hellhound struggled furiously to reach him. Taking a gamble, Fargo kicked it. The beast yelped and pulled back. Another moment, and Devy was there, staggering under her burden. Fargo took another gamble. He let go of the doors long enough to grab the bar and shove it into place, wedging it securely.

The hellhounds continued to hurl themselves at the stable doors.

Snatching up the Henry, Fargo shot through the door at where the growls were loudest and was rewarded with a yip. Just like that, the sounds stopped. He peered through the crack between the doors but the pack had vanished.

Devy was with Gwen, who was sobbing hysterically. Holding her, the mother said softly, "Hush, little one. Everything will be all right. I won't let them do to you what they did to your pa."

Fargo remembered seeing a hay door in the loft. He climbed the ladder and went over and knelt. It had a small latch. Careful not to show himself, he slowly pushed the door open. The street was deserted but he doubted the hellhounds had left. His hunch was confirmed when two hybrids came from near the saloon and were joined by two others from across the street. One was the huge leader. They were searching for prey, he suspected.

Three more appeared. Tongues lolling, they joined the rest. A female was limping. When Fargo shot through the door, he had hit her in the hip. She was bleeding profusely. He noticed that she hung back from the rest as if afraid to be too close.

The leader raised his broad head and sniffed. He looked at the female, at the blood flowing from the hole in her hip, and she bared her teeth and growled. He lowered his head and began to circle her. The others took that as a cue to fan out and hem her in. The female never took her eyes off the leader. He stopped a few yards away and raised his head and sniffed again.

The female shifted to face him. The instant she did, the leader pounced. He was on her before she could set herself. His shoulder smashed into her hurt hip and she was bowled over. She tried to scramble up but the big male was merciless. His jaws clamped onto her neck, shearing deep. She whined and held herself still but it did no good. With a powerful wrench, the leader tore half her throat out. Death was instantaneous. The rest tore into her before her legs stopped thrashing, ripping and rending.

Fargo watched a while, then sat back. Everything Devy had told him about the hellhounds was true. They were as vicious as vicious could be. Far more so than the coyotes and dogs that sired them. And to think, there were thirty more of those things running around loose. As if there were not enough to worry about with the drought and the rabies.

Fargo shut the hay door and climbed down. Devona and Gwen were huddled in a corner, the girl sniffling. "We're all right for now. They can't get in." To be doubly sure he double-checked the rear door to be certain that it was shut and bolted. There weren't any windows.

"Thank you for saving us," Devy said quietly when he went to the front to peek out. "I didn't mean to cause you any trouble. I'm worried about my son, is all."

The hellhounds were ripping at the female with savage zeal. Fargo would let them feast a while yet. The more they ate, they more sluggish they would be. "How old is your boy?"

"Fourteen."

"Then he's old enough to take care of himself," Fargo commented. West of the Mississippi, most boys that age were doing the work of grown men. By sixteen many struck off on their own.

"Billy is mature, I'll grant you that," Devy said fondly. "He's done of lot of growing since his pa died. Physically and emotionally. But he's alone and he needs me and it tears me apart not to be there."

"It's my fault, Ma," Gwen stopped sniffling to say. "I never should have run off like I did."

"We needed food," Devy justified the deed. "I'd have done the same thing if I were in your shoes."

"You would?" The girl smiled and hugged her mother closer. "You're the best ma in the whole world."

Fargo climbed the ladder to the hayloft. Sinking onto his stomach, he crawled to the hay door and opened it as carefully as before. All the hellhounds except one were on their bellies, ringing the female, their snouts buried in her flesh. The exception was the leader. He had stopped eating and was staring at the stable.

Slowly tucking the Henry to his shoulder, Fargo fixed a bead on the leader's broad chest. Fate had given him a golden chance to thin their ranks. He would start with the dominant male and drop as many of the others as he could before they reached cover.

As if it sensed what Fargo was about to do, the leader suddenly raced off between two buildings. Some of the remaining hounds raised their heads and looked around.

Fargo shifted the Henry to the second largest. He sighted on a point between its ears and blew its brains out with a clean stroke of the trigger. The rest instantly leaped to their feet and bolted. He shot one that turned broadside, shot another in midstride, shot a third nearing the corner of the general store. He worked the lever again but there were no more to shoot. Two besides the leader had gotten away.

He waited a while, hoping one would poke its head out, but they were crafty, these hybrids. They learned from their mistakes. He bolted the small door and descended.

"How many?" Devy asked.

Fargo held up four fingers. Four out of forty wasn't a lot but it was four less sets of fangs and claws, and that was what counted. "When we're sure the others have gone, we'll head for your farm."

"How will we know?"

"I doubt they'll stick around long. After while I'll

go out and look around." Fargo figured an hour before sunset would be best.

Devy gnawed on her lower lip. "I don't suppose I could convince you to let us go by ourselves?"

"You want to die, is that it?" Fargo didn't know what to make of her. She was devoted to her children yet she was willing to put herself and her youngest at enormous risk unnecessarily.

"I don't want to impose."

"That line won't wash twice," Fargo said bluntly. "But if you want, I'll take you as far as your farm and be on my way." He nodded toward Gwen, whose eyes were closed and whose chin was drooping. "For her sake you should think twice about making a go of it alone."

Devy began to say something but changed her mind and lapsed into silence. Soon both she and her little girl were asleep.

Fargo was feeling drowsy, himself. It was the heat. It was enough to sap anyone's vitality. He sat with his back to the Ovaro's stall, facing the double doors, the Henry across his lap. Staying awake proved impossible. He dozed in snatches, jerking his head up at the slightest sounds. Once he thought he heard a shout. Another time it was breaking glass.

The afternoon waned. Fargo had drifted off again when another noise snapped his head up. It was a growl from right outside. He dashed to the crack but couldn't see what made it. Something scratched at the outer wall to his left, and he heard it move around to the east. It was circling the stable.

Fargo raised the Henry, then lowered it again. The Carroways were still sleeping. He shadowed the stalker, moving when it moved, stopping when it stopped. He was sure it was a hellhound, probably the leader. When it came to the pump it sniffed loudly a few times. He thought it would slip through the corral rails and prowl along the back wall to the back door but he did not hear it again after that.

Fargo went to the loft and looked out. The dead hellhounds lay where they had fallen. Holding onto the edge, he leaned out. For as far as the eye could see, the brown hills lay still under the fiery red of the setting sun. He started to pull himself back in, and froze.

Out of nowhere a man had appeared at the end of the street. He was in his thirties, perhaps older. His black hair was in need of a combing and he could stand to have a shave. His clothes were filthy. He had no shoes or boots.

Fargo waved to get the man's attention but the man had already seen him and was heading toward the stable. He opened his mouth to warn about the hellhounds but the shout died in his throat.

The man had the same stiff-legged gait as the red fox. Spasms racked him every few steps and his face constantly twitched. In his right hand he clasped a bloody axe. As he lurched abreast of the dead hellhounds, he halted and hacked at one until he severed the head from the body. Then, picking up the dripping head, he stared into the hellhound's eyes, tittered insanely, walked over to an empty horse trough, and dropped the head in.

The straw behind Fargo rustled. Instinctively, he whirled, but it was only Devona Carroway. Her nap had restored color to her cheeks. "Sorry if I startled you. Gwen is still asleep. I thought I would come up and see what you were doing."

"We have company." Fargo slid aside so she could see out.

"Dear God." Devy slid to the opening, her shoulder brushing his. "That's Pete Spence. He's the town barber. I haven't seen him in weeks. Why is he walking like that?" Comprehension dawned and she swayed. "No. Not Pete, too. He was such a kind, gentle soul."

Not anymore. Spence hobbled up to the stable doors, his face lit by a maniacal inner glow. He laughed to himself, the laughter punctuated by gurgles and grunts.

Fargo raised the Henry.

"No! You can't!" Devy grabbed the barrel. "Let him be and he'll wander off. He can't hurt us."

"You're forgetting the axe," Fargo reminded her, and hardly had he done so than the stable doors shook to a solid blow.

From under the hayloft came a scream.

"Gwen!" Devy cried. Maternal love swept her to the ladder. She flew down, her dress hiking up above her knees.

Fargo leaned out of the hay door. Spence delivered several more blows, the axe biting deep into the wood. Given time he would break through. Fargo pointed the Henry straight down. "I'm sorry it has to be this way, mister."

Spence's head snapped up. An inhuman growl tore from his throat and he clawed at the wall in a vain bid to climb it. Froth forming on his lower lip, he let out with a bestial howl.

It was answered from down the street.

Fargo could not say whether the answering howl came from a human throat or a hellhound. He looked but saw nothing. Placing his cheek to the Henry, he prepared to put Pete Spence out of his misery. Only the barber was no longer there. He was going around the corner.

Concerned the rabid madman might circle around to the back and try to break in there, Fargo hurried down.

Devy and Gwen were huddled by the stalls. The girl couldn't stop crying and the mother was trying to comfort her.

The rear of the stable was quiet. Fargo put an ear to the door but didn't hear anything. He stayed there a while to be sure, then rejoined the Carroways and announced, "We have a decision to make."

"If you mean whether to try for my farm or wait out the night here, you know how I'll vote," Devy said.

"The hellhounds could still be out there. Your friend the barber, too."

"So? There's no guarantee they'll drift elsewhere before dawn. We should go right this minute, while there's still light left. Pete won't be able to catch us and your rifle will keep the hellhounds at bay."

"Your husband's rifle didn't," Fargo observed, and Devona winced as if he had punched her.

"All that matters to me is that my son is alone and needs me. I'm going to him whether you tag along or not." Devy smiled. "I won't hold it against you if you decide to stay. It's a lot safer in here than it will be out there." She patted Gwen's head. "I'd leave her with you but she won't stay, and nothing in this world can stop this child when she puts her mind to something."

"Just so we're clear it's your idea." Fargo brought the stallion out of the stall and placed the bridle on. Next he slid on the saddle blanket. Holding the saddle by the gullet and the cantle, he swung it up and over. Then he stuck two fingers under the blanket where it lay over the withers and raised the blanket a bit. Placing the left stirrup up over the saddle horn, he reached under the Ovaro for the cinch.

"A lot of men wouldn't go to all the trouble you are for a couple of strangers," Devy commented.

"So?" Fargo had never been one to run with the herd, to do what everyone else was doing. He had his own life to live and he would live it as he saw fit, and anyone who didn't like it could take a short walk off a tall cliff.

"I never did catch your name."

Fargo introduced himself. Soon he was cinched up and ready, the Henry in the saddle scabbard, the canned goods crammed into his saddlebags. He led the pinto to the double doors.

Devy carried Gwen to the horse. Tears had left brown streaks on the girl's dirty cheeks. She smiled sweetly and stared at the Ovaro, her tiny fingers raveling and unraveling her mother's hair. "He's mighty big, mister."

"That's so I can see over the tops of trees," Fargo

36

replied, sparking a peal of laughter, the first he'd heard the girl voice.

"You're joshing. No horse is that big." Gwen's smile faded. "My pa had a nice horse. We called it Andy after Andy Jackson, a president my pa admired. Those mean hellhounds killed it, just like they did him." She stared into his eyes. "You're not going to let them kill us, are you?"

"Not if I can help it." Fargo wouldn't make promises he couldn't keep. "You hang on tight and do exactly as I say."

"How soon?" Devy asked.

Fargo peeked out the crack. Timing was crucial. Too soon, and there would be too much light, and the hellhounds or the rabid barber might spot them. Too late, and they would not have light enough to see if they were being pursued. It had to be during the few minutes when twilight shaded into full night.

The sun was below the horizon.

"Climb on," Fargo told the mother.

Devy gripped the saddle horn and pulled herself up. "Seat or back?"

"Back," Fargo answered, "with the girl between us." The mother would be responsible for the daughter. He needed his hands free for the reins or his Colt or both.

Nodding, Devy slid back past the cantle, leaving enough space for Gwen. Fargo handed her up and Devy wrapped both arms tight. "Don't you worry, darling. Before you know it we'll be home and everything will be fine."

Gwen was young but she wasn't stupid. "No it won't, Ma. Nothing will ever be fine again."

Fargo turned to the doors. The street was still deserted. He wanted to fill his canteen but the pump made too much noise. "If something should happen to me," he mentioned without looking at them, "take my horse and ride." He thought of a question he should have asked sooner. "How far to your farm?"

"About four miles. It's not much. Just the house and a barn and a chicken coop, but my husband built well. We were always so proud of it."

The twilight deepened rapidly. Fargo gripped the bar, his every nerve on edge. The moment came. With as little noise as possible, he raised the bar and set it to one side. He pushed on the doors, spun, and was in the saddle before the doors stopped swinging. He had to watch his spurs when he slid his leg over so as not to jab Gwen. Her small hands hooked onto his gun belt and one of Devy's gripped his shoulder. He lifted the reins.

Out of the gloom shambled a hideous mockery of a human being. Pete Spence's mouth was rimmed with spittle and his nose was bleeding. Clutching the axe, he planted himself in their path.

Gwen had not seen the apparition but Devy's fingernails bit into Fargo's skin and she gasped.

Lashing the Ovaro's reins, Fargo rode directly at him. At the last instant he reined wide, slipped his boot from its stirrup, and kicked. His foot connected with the axe handle as the axe arced toward the pinto. Spence was knocked to the ground. Another flick of the reins and they were in the clear.

Fargo reined to the southeast and brought the Ovaro to a trot. A glance showed Pete Spence stumbling after them but they were well beyond his reach and widening their lead with every stride of the stallion's sturdy legs.

Darkness enfolded them. Fargo leaned forward so the girl wouldn't be squeezed between him and her mother. Devy's hand was still on his shoulder but nearer his neck. He shut the warm feel of her palm from his mind and devoted himself to the terrain. It was flat and grassy until the first hill. The slope was steep but not so steep Devy couldn't stay on. At the top Fargo slowed and rose in the stirrups to look back. Carn was mired in darkling shadows. Not a light gleamed anywhere. He watched the field where it met the town.

From out of the shadows, across the slightly lighter brown of the grass, sped low, swift forms.

"Damn," Fargo said, and used his spurs.

"What's wrong?" Devona asked.

Hellhounds were after them.

4

Skye Fargo faced a dilemma. Ordinarily, the Ovaro would easily outdistance the hybrids. But because of the woman and her child, riding at a full gallop was out of the question; they might be unhorsed. Eventually the hellhounds would catch up, and Fargo had to think of something before that happened.

Rolling hills were on all sides, some sprinkled with vegetation, some without. Fargo could not tell much else in the dark. A minute more, and out of the night reared the highest hill yet. It was bare clear to the top, and acting on a sudden idea, Fargo reined up it.

"What are you doing?" Devy Carroway had to raise her voice to be heard. "Our farm is a long ways off yet."

At the top Fargo sprang down, shucked the Henry, and put a hand on the woman's shapely leg. "Hellhounds," he succinctly explained. "Be ready. If they get past me, ride like hell." Palming the Colt, he pressed it into her hand. "Use this if you have to." He took a step but small fingers gripped the whangs on his sleeve.

"Mr. Fargo?"

"Yes?" The girl's face was pale in the starlight.

"Be careful. I like you."

Fargo smiled, ran ten feet down the slope, and dropped to one knee. The hybrids had to be following by scent and that scent would bring them right to him.

He would have one chance and one chance only. He must not let them get past.

From out of the darkness wafted a piercing howl.

Fargo could use the eyesight of an owl right about now. Or a mountain lion. Both saw better at night than he did. He concentrated on where the grass and the dark merged, his cheek against the Henry. They did not keep him waiting.

A pair of swift shapes bounded up the slope. Their heads were to the ground and they were breathing heavily from their long run. The one in the lead looked up and snarled.

Fargo fired and the first hybrid went down. As he jacked the lever he shifted the barrel to the second. It came right for him, a growl rumbling from its chest, its teeth gleaming white. The Henry banged and it stumbled but it didn't fall. He fired again and it stumbled again but it stayed on its feet, and now it was almost to him, its mouth yawning wide to bite. He fired when its muzzle was only inches from the Henry's and the hellhound collapsed in its tracks, its fangs practically brushing his boot.

"Look out!" Devona cried.

A third hellhound was closing fast. Fargo squeezed the trigger and the slug snapped the beast around but didn't stop it. They were tough, these hybrids, all iron and fire and sheer raw savagery. He shot it when it was eight feet away but it surged onto its paws and he shot it once more when it was four feet away. At the same time his Colt blasted, almost in his ear. The two slugs punched the hellhound onto its side and it thrashed a moment and went limp.

Fargo rose and turned. "You didn't stay on the horse like I told you."

"I couldn't let you do it alone." Devy handed him the smoking Colt. "Gwen isn't the only one who likes you."

Digesting that, Fargo followed her to the Ovaro. He slid the Henry into the scabbard, then gave her a boost up.

Gwen was all smiles. "You got them! Just like you got that fox and Mr. Strum. You're awful good at killing things."

"I've had a lot of practice." Fargo took hold of the saddle horn and climbed on.

"You might get more sooner than you want," Devy mentioned. "Those shots will carry quite a ways. More hellhounds might show up."

"Then we'll be somewhere else when they get here." Fargo descended the hill. Once at the bottom he trotted southeast. The girl had both arms around his waist and the mother had both hands on his shoulders. After a while one of Devy's hands shifted to his neck. Her skin was soft to the touch.

Out of the blue she asked, "Have you ever lost anyone you cared for?"

"Who hasn't?" Fargo did not tell her about the deaths of his parents when he was young, or about the friends and loved ones he had lost since.

"I don't want to lose another one. Keep that in mind, will you?"

Fargo thought he knew what she was getting at. "I'll do my best to protect your daughter."

"And Billy," Gwen piped up. "Don't forget my brother."

"And Billy," Fargo assured her.

The countryside was as quiet as a graveyard. Missing were the yips of coyotes, the occasional screams of cougars, and all the grunts and shrieks and wails that made the night come alive. Only the howls of hellhounds were heard, now from the east, later the north, still later the west.

"I hope they don't find us," Gwen said.

After a couple of miles Fargo slowed to a walk. He was sweating as if it were day. By his best reckoning, the temperature had fallen only to the lower nineties and the air was thick and humid. "Is there water on this property of yours?"

"We have a well but it went dry weeks ago," Devy said. "I stored jars of water in the root cellar before-

42

hand and there are a few left to tide us over, if that's what you're thinking."

Fargo was thinking of the Ovaro. "Tomorrow we should head for the Snake River. I can take you to Fort Bridger from there. You can get all the help you need."

"Ma?" Gwen said.

"Hush, child."

That was the last anyone spoke until Fargo rounded a wooded hill and a narrow valley unfolded before them. Midway across stood several buildings flanked by trees. A putrid odor wafted on the breeze. The source lay scattered here and there, dark humps resembling tombstones.

"All our cows are dead or missing," Devy told him. "The drought wiped us out like it did everyone else."

"Why did you stay on after your husband died?" To Fargo that would have been the time to pack up and leave.

"It's our home." Devona paused. "If you've ever had a place of your own you would understand. A house is more than lumber and nails. A farm is more than grass and water. Your home becomes a part of you. Turning your back on it is hard."

Both the barn and a chicken coop were to the left of the house. Fargo reined in and dismounted. "Shouldn't you let your son know we're here?" The windows were dark and there was no sign of anyone.

"I would imagine he knows," Devy said softly.

Simultaneously, from the chicken coop, keened a high-pitched screech. The door shook and rattled, as if something inside were trying to break out.

Whirling, Fargo drew his Colt. "Stay here." He hadn't taken four steps when Gwen's small hands gripped his.

"No! Don't hurt him! Please!" She tugged on his arm to try to stop him, leaning her whole body back. "He can't help how he is."

Fargo looked down. "He? Do you mean that's your brother?"

Devy walked past them. "Billy has rabies. He was bit by a bat about two weeks ago. I did what I could but now he's half out of his mind." She glanced at Gwen. "Let go of him, little one."

"Why didn't you tell me sooner?" Fargo trailed along, the Colt still in his hand. The boy had stopped shaking the door but from the coop issued growls worthy of a hellhound.

"I didn't know how you would take it. When the rabies first started, those who came down with it were shot on sight."

"You thought I would shoot him?"

"Leon Hinkle would. From the very start he's been out to kill every rabid animal and person he finds." Devy gazed north. "He hasn't been by in a while so maybe he's stopped searching or the hellhounds got him."

The chicken coop shook to another burst of violence. It withstood the assault, a bar on the outside of the door jiggling.

"Don't worry," Devy said. "He can't get out. Brian made it too well. He was a great carpenter."

"What about the chickens?" Fargo hadn't heard any squawk.

"Gone. I left the door open the night after Brian died. I wasn't thinking straight. And something got in with them. A coon, a fox, I don't really know, but it killed every last one. Bit their heads clean off but only ate the rooster."

Fargo had heard of predators doing that. A killing frenzy came over them, and they slaughtered far more than they could eat. In Wyoming Territory a year ago, a mountain lion leaped a fence into a sheep pen and killed thirty-four. In Colorado, nine cows in a pasture fell to a grizzly's paws but none were eaten.

Devy placed her hand on the bar. "Billy? It's your mother? If you understand me, please say something."

More growls were her answer. Blows rained on the inside of the door but it held.

Gwen was crying. "Ma, I can't stand him like this. Isn't there anything we can do? Anything at all?"

"Only one thing." Devy looked at Fargo's Colt. "And I'm not ready to do that yet. They say rabies takes ten to twelve days to run its course, and he's not at the worst of it yet."

"It gets worse?" Gwen raised her tear-filled eyes to Fargo. "How can God let this happen, mister? My pa always said God looks after us. He read us stories about how good God is. But God let my pa die and now Billy will die and there's nothing we can do. Why, mister? Why?"

"You're asking the wrong person. I don't have the answers any more than you do." Fargo turned. "I'm going to bed down my horse."

The barn was half the size of the stable. It had six stalls and one feed trough. Fargo took his time stripping the Ovaro. He heard the boy snarl and hiss, and the mother's low, insistent voice as she sought to soothe the savagery that raged in her son's ravaged mind and body.

His saddlebags over his shoulder, Fargo closed the barn door and walked to the house. From the porch he could see the length and breadth of the valley. Brian Carroway had chosen well. It was a pocket of paradise. Or had been until all hell broke loose.

The screen door opened soundlessly when Fargo pulled. The inner door had a glass pane and fluffy curtains on the inside. Fargo's spurs jingled as he walked down a hardwood hallway to the kitchen. It was hot and stifling. He opened a window to let in what little breeze there was.

Candles were in a cabinet above the stove. Fargo lit several and placed them where their flickering glow bathed the entire kitchen and noticed that a skillet and pots and pans were stacked neatly next to a basin. From his saddlebags he took the canned goods. He pried one of the large cans of Van Camp's pork and beans open and poured the contents into a pan. Lighting the stove was no problem. A box of wood and kindling sat beside it.

Fargo laid out three plates, forks and spoons. He set out three glasses, opened the canned cow, and filled each glass halfway. Once the beans started to bubble, he stirred them. When they had cooked long enough, he removed the pan from the burner. He was ladling the beans onto the plates when footsteps filled the hallway and Devona appeared, carrying Gwen.

"Oh my."

"I figured you might be hungry." Fargo set the pan down. "There are peaches for dessert."

Gwen leaped from her mother's arms. "Food, Ma! Food!" She pulled out a chair and hopped up. "Hurry and sit down! My tummy is trying to climb into my mouth, I'm so hungry."

Devy had not taken her eyes off Fargo. "This is very thoughtful. I can't thank you enough."

"No need." Fargo held out a chair.

"Thank you, kind sir." She flushed pink in the cheeks as she sat down.

"Don't forget grace, Ma," Gwen said.

Devona folded her hands. The candlelight enhanced her beauty. It erased the worry lines and the fatigue and showed her as she must have been before the ordeal started.

Fargo could understand why Brian Carroway asked for her hand in marriage. She was lovely. He kept his thoughts to himself, though, and ate slowly to make it last longer.

Not Gwen. She gobbled her beans and peaches and gulped her milk, then sat back with a huge grin and patted her stomach. "I'm so full I could bust. We haven't eaten this good in weeks."

"You ate too fast. We're not half finished yet."

Gwen tried to stifle a yawn but failed. "I'm terribly tired, Ma. Do you suppose you could tuck me in?"

"I'd be glad to." Devy set down her spoon. "You've had a long day, little miss. You snuck off at dawn, if you'll recall." She pushed back her chair and stood. "Come on. Tonight you sleep in your own bed instead of the parlor as we have been doing."

"Is it safe, Ma?"

The mother glanced at Fargo. "Yes, it's very safe. I'll be up a while yet but I'll look in on you before I turn in."

Devona was a long time coming back down. She had changed into a clean dress and brushed her hair. When she entered the kitchen, she brought with her the musky scent of perfume. She didn't look at Fargo as she reclaimed her seat and resumed eating. "Gwen sure does like you. She wouldn't stop chattering about how nice you are."

"Don't let her get too attached. I'll be riding on as soon as the two of you are safe."

The spoon stopped halfway to Devy's mouth. "I figured as much. But that's later and this is now, and I'm a grown woman and can do as I please."

"Just so you know." Fargo sipped his milk and studied her over the rim of the glass. Her sandy hair had lustrous blonde tints to it, her lips were full and ripe. She was not overly endowed above the waist but she wasn't flat, either. She had a slim waist and those long legs, legs any man would love to have wrapped around him.

"Six months is a long time to do without."

Fargo leaned back and laced his fingers behind his head. He had to admire her frankness. "That it is."

"You're an extremely handsome man, Skye. Brian wasn't all that handsome but he was dependable. I think that's why I married him, more than anything else. He was always so dependable until he went and got himself killed."

"Maybe we shouldn't talk about it."

"His mistake was staying in town so late. He didn't do it often, but one of the few times he did, it cost him." Devy rested her forehead on her wrist. "It's the little mistakes that cost us the most, isn't it?"

Fargo felt uncomfortable talking about her husband. "You can't blame him. We never know when our string has played out."

"I don't blame him. I blame life. It's a hard, cruel world in which we live, and that's the honest truth. The best we can do is ward the cruelty off until our time comes to be planted."

"Where will you go from here?" Fargo changed the subject when she wouldn't.

"Nowhere. What makes you think I would make a sham of all the work and energy Brian and I put into this place? Eventually the drought will end and the rabies will run its course and life will go back to normal."

"And the hellhounds?"

"The rabies will claim most, I should think. Those it doesn't will be hunted down and exterminated." Devy had it all worked out. "We have some money squirreled away. Not much, but enough for half a dozen head of cattle and some chickens. I'll start over. Who knows? Maybe one day another man will come along who is as dependable as Brian was."

In the distance a hellhound howled. "Did you bolt the front door when you came in?" Fargo asked her.

"I'm not sure."

"I'd better check." His Henry in hand, Fargo walked down the hall. He threw the bolt, but instead of returning to the kitchen, he went into the parlor and sat on the settee. It faced a window that afforded a view of the barn and the chicken coop and the hills to the north. Leaning the Henry against the wall, he sat back, letting the tension drain from his body.

Fargo closed his eyes. He was tired and sore and his side hurt from where the pitchfork had gouged him. He could use some sleep but he should stay up a while to be sure they were out of danger. His eyelids drooped once, twice, three times, and without intending to, he dozed off. A subtle sound awakened him. The flowery fragrance of perfume tingled his nose as he sat up.

Devona stood before him. Her hair hung partly over her face, hiding her expression. Her long legs were set wide apart as if to steady herself, and her hands were on her thighs. "She's asleep. I just checked."

Not yet fully awake, Fargo said, "There are peaches left in the can if you want more dessert."

"I had something else in mind." Devy straddled his knees, facing him. "I hope you won't think I'm a hussy."

"Hussies are some of my best friends," Fargo responded, and she grinned. He put his hands on her hips and kneaded them, and she shivered and arched her back. Slowly bending toward him, she paused.

"I don't have a lot of experience at this. You'll have to excuse me if I'm a little nervous."

"You're excused." Fargo kissed her. Her mouth was exquisitely soft, wonderfully moist. He entwined his tongue with hers and she squirmed on his lap. Her hands rose to his hair and she removed his hat and dropped it to the floor.

"You kiss marvelously," Devy breathlessly complimented him when they parted. "Something tells me you've had a lot of practice."

"Not all that much," Fargo replied. Which was like saying the Rockies were not all that high. He kissed her again. This time he covered her left breast with his hand, and squeezed. She cooed deep in her throat. He felt her nipple harden through the fabric and pinched it.

"Ohhhhh." Devy gripped him by the hair and pressed herself hard against him. "I felt a tingle clear down to my toes."

"You'll feel more," Fargo promised, and covered her other breast while inhaling her tongue into his mouth. She ground her hips, her thighs closing tight on his legs. Her nails scraped the back of his neck as she roved them to his shoulders and down his arms. He pried at the tiny buttons on her dress to gain access to her concealed charms and presently bared both breasts.

Devy moaned when Fargo glued his mouth to a nipple. Her hips writhed and she scooted her bottom closer to the bulge in his buckskin pants. He flicked the nipple with the tip of his tongue, nipped it lightly with his front teeth. He licked around and around until her breast was lathered. Then he did the same to her other heaving mound.

"You—you—" Devona husked, but she did not finish her comment. She ran her fingers from his back to his belt.

Fargo slid his right hand across her hip and down her thigh almost to her knee. Her dress was bunched above it, and he slowly slid his fingers under the hem. She stiffened as his hand traveled up her smooth thigh to the junction of those superbly long legs of hers.

"I want you," Devy whispered.

"So I noticed." Fargo worked his fingers through her underthings to her bush. She groaned at the contact. He slid his middle finger lower, across her womanhood, and inserted it between her moist nether lips. But only for a moment, only enough to tantalize her with the prospect of more pleasure to come.

"You're only the second man I've ever been with. I should be ashamed of myself but I'm not. Is that wrong?"

Fargo wished she would shut up and kiss him.

Suddenly Devy did. She feverishly kissed his face all over; his forehead, his eyebrows, his eyes, his cheeks, his nose, his chin. Quick, hot kisses, that did not seem as if they would ever end.

Fargo touched her swollen knob and Devy exhaled loudly, a sigh to end all sighs. He lightly brushed his finger back and forth and each time her breathing became a degree heavier, her thighs clamped a degree tighter.

"What you do to me," Devy whispered.

When Fargo suddenly slid his finger up into her, she arched her back and opened her mouth as if to cry out, but didn't. She didn't want to wake Gwen, he realized. Nor did he, although his reason was more selfish; to avoid having their lovemaking interrupted.

Devy's fingers plucked at his gun belt. She could not undo it fast enough. Once she did, she unfastened his pants, freeing his member. Her mouth formed an oval and her eyes grew hooded with lust. "I see that you and that big stallion of yours have something in common."

Now it was Fargo who groaned. She stroked him, cupped him, delicately traced a finger up and around. He bore it as long as he could. Then he gripped her by the hips and raised her high enough to slide his pole up under her parted thighs. Smiling seductively, she helped align herself.

Fargo lowered her inch by gradual inch. It was like sheathing his sword in a satin scabbard. When he was buried all the way, he paused. Their eyes met. He began to thrust, she to grind herself against him. Her wet walls clung like satin, eliciting pleasure beyond measure.

Their tempo quickened. Fargo thrust harder and harder and Devona ground herself faster and faster. The settee creaked under them. Suddenly her head snapped back, her fingernails buried in his biceps, and she gushed.

"Oh! Yes! Yes!"

Her release triggered Fargo's. The parlor exploded in dazzling pinpoints of light. He floated as if on thin air, cast adrift from himself, and for a while all was right with the world. For a while the drought and the rabies epidemic and the hellhounds were forgotten. For a while there was only the two of them, lying spent in each other's arms.

Then a howl rent the night, from near the barn, and the Ovaro uttered a strident whinny.

5

Skye Fargo's all too brief respite was over. He would rather have enjoyed a night of peace and quiet but it was not to be. Sliding Devy off, he hastily hitched his pants and strapped on his gun belt. He grabbed the Henry, threw the bolt to the front door, and ran onto the porch. Devy called his name but he didn't slow or stop. Not when the Ovaro was in danger.

Like hostile warriors circling a wagon train, lupine shadows were circling the barn. Fargo saw one clawing at the barn door. He centered the Henry's sights on it and stroked the trigger. The hellhound yipped, leaped straight up into the air, turned upside down, and did not move again after it hit the ground.

In a twinkling the other hellhounds bounded toward him.

Fargo dropped one, levered another round into the Henry's chamber, and shot another. He could not get them all before they reached him. There were too many and they were coming too fast. Firing nonstop, he backpedaled.

"Hurry!" Devy cried. She held the front door open.

Fargo still had a few feet to cover when hybrid paws clacked on the porch. A slavering hellhound was about to spring. Twisting, he fired from the hip just as the beast launched itself at him. The impact of the slug catapulted it into the onrushing jaws of its fellow halfbloods, slowing them enough for Fargo to make it inside and for Devy to slam the door shut.

Upstairs, Gwen was screaming.

"Go to her!" Fargo shouted, and gave Devy a shove toward the stairs. As he faced the door a hellhound crashed against the glass, shattering it into a thousand shards that showered across the floor like rain. He flung an arm in front of his face to protect his eyes, and when he lowered it, the hellhound was partway through and clawing at the jamb. It snapped at him, its fangs gnashing.

Fargo shot the beast between the eyes and it sagged, lifeless, half in and half out. He began to shove it out but decided to leave it hanging there to keep the others from getting in.

The pack was making enough racket to be heard in Carn. Fargo saw several outside of the wide window, and for a few harrowing seconds he thought they would crash through it as the other had the door. But they ran on around to the side of the house, perhaps looking for another way to gain entry.

Fargo raced to the kitchen for the box of ammunition in his saddlebags. As he reloaded he heard hellhounds sniffing and growling at the back door. He went down the hall to the stairs and up to the second floor. Devy was on the edge of a bed, holding Gwen. Fargo entered the room across the hall and rushed to a front window.

Hellhounds milled below. He saw none near the barn but spotted a few near the chicken coop. Unlatching a window, he slid it open. Some of the hybrids heard and looked up. Snarling furiously, they leaped at him but fell far short. He shot one, shot another, killed a third, and then the rest broke and scattered. He sent a shot after one slower than the others and it pitched forward but regained its feet and scurried into the darkness.

At the chicken coop two hybrids were clawing at the door. If he fired at them there was too great a risk of a bullet going through the door and hitting the boy, so he shot into the ground next to them. They kept clawing at the coop.

Fargo whirled. The coop door might hold, it might not. He was down the stairs and to the front door before his mind caught up with his feet. He shoved the dead hellhound outside, opened the door, and ran to the end of the porch. Where the chicken coop door should be was a black rectangle. They had broken it down.

"No," Fargo breathed, thinking of the mother and the girl. He charged across the yard.

Out of the coop spilled Billy Carroway and a hellhound, locked in savage struggle. They rolled back and forth, limbs and bodies entwined.

Fargo figured the boy would be getting the worst of it but he saw, to his amazement, that it was Billy who had his teeth buried in the hellhound's throat and was tearing at the hellhound's jugular.

A second hybrid hurtled from the coop. Almost too late, Fargo smashed it to the earth with a pair of swift shots. He dashed closer to try and help the boy and was nearly bowled over when, in their wild thrashing about, they rolled toward his legs. Leaping aside, he awaited his chance. Using the Henry was momentarily out of the question. He might hit the boy.

A cry of anguish from the porch added an unwanted element. Devy was there, Gwen in her arms.

"Stay back!" Fargo shouted, but she ignored him. He turned to the fight in time to see the boy rip the hellhound's throat open. The beast went limp and Billy Carroway rose. Blood caked his mouth and chin, mixed with the froth that rimmed his lips. His fingers hooking into claws, he came toward Fargo.

"Billy, no!" Devona darted between them and thrust out an arm. "Please, for the love of heaven, don't do this!"

Once, Billy Carroway had been a dutiful son who dearly loved his parents. Once, he had been a normal boy who liked to laugh and play and do all the things boys everywhere loved to do. The rabies had turned him into a mindless brute as fierce as the hellhounds. Hydrophobia had him in its unrelenting grip. An overpowering urge dominated him, an impulse to attack anything and everything, including his own mother and sister.

Stepping to the right to have a clear line of fire, Fargo waited until the last possible instant, until the boy was about to seize his mother and sink his teeth into her. Then he fired, once.

Devy was frozen speechless. Gwen, thankfully, had her face buried in her mother's bosom and did not witness her brother's grisly end.

"Get inside," Fargo urged. The rest of the hellhounds were still around and might attack at any moment.

"You shot him!" Without warning, Devona flailed at him with her free hand. "You shot my son! I hate you! I hate you! I hate you!"

Fargo grabbed her wrist and held fast. Tears were streaming down her cheeks and and she was shaking like an aspen leaf. She blinked, then moaned, and sagged against him. Wrapping an arm around her waist, Fargo steered her toward the house. He felt bad about the boy but it had to be done and that was that.

Mother and daughter bawled the entire way in and were still bawling when Fargo set them on the settee. "Stay here," he said, and went back out. From up the valley wafted howls.

Jogging to the barn, he pulled on the big door. The Ovaro welcomed him with a nicker. He slid its bridle on and led the stallion from the stall. Devona might not like what he was about to do but he was not leaving the stallion there.

The stallion balked at climbing the steps to the porch but did after some coaxing. One of the boards cracked under the weight but the Ovaro's leg didn't go through. Fargo had to press on its neck to get it to duck its head so it could make it through the door-way. It was a tight squeeze. He led it a dozen feet down the hall.

Dabbing at her eyes with a sleeve, Devy came up off the settee. "What in the world are you up to?"

"The hellhounds broke into the chicken coop, they

might try to break into the barn. Without my horse we won't stand a prayer of making it to the river." Fargo shut the door, leaned the Henry against the wall, and walked to a china cabinet. The cabinet was heavy, but by sliding first one side forward and then the other, he positioned it with its back flush against the front door. "That should keep them out."

"You think of everything." Devy averted her eyes. "I'm sorry for what I said out there. Terribly sorry. I didn't mean it. I can't hate you for doing what I should have done days ago if I had the courage."

Fargo squeezed her shoulder. "Take Gwen upstairs. I'll keep watch." Bent in misery, they trudged to the stairs. He conducted a check of the ground-floor windows. From each he scoured the valley and the hills but the hellhounds were nowhere to be found.

The Ovaro was taking the change calmly enough. Fargo had been concerned the wood floor might not take the stallion's great weight, but as Devona was so proud of saying, her husband had built well. The floor creaked a lot but none of the boards gave way.

With everything done that he could do for the time being, Fargo slid the settee closer to the window but turned it so its back was to the pane. That way, the hellhounds wouldn't spot him if they looked in. For over an hour he sat up, listening and watching. The valley lay quiet under the stars. Convinced the hellhounds were gone, he stretched out with his boots over one end and his head propped in his hands.

It must have been past midnight when Fargo drifted asleep. His was a fitful rest. Even though no sounds intruded on his slumber, again and again he awoke with a start, plagued by a sense of unease. Half an hour before sunrise he was up and made another check of the house. He went upstairs and peeked in on the Carroways. They were out to the world; physical and emotional exhaustion had taken its toll. He decided to let them sleep as long as they needed to, and closed the bedroom door.

Sunrise was less spectacular than usual. A heat haze

hung thick over the parched region, dulling the sun's radiance. It lent the landscape a strange and alien aspect, and gave Fargo the illusion he was gazing at a painting like those he had seen in a gallery in St. Louis. A far away howl proved otherwise.

Sliding the china cabinet to one side, Fargo ventured outdoors. The heat was already stifling. He went from one end of the porch to the other. Now and again he caught a whiff of rotting cow carcasses. He would like to dispose of them for Devy's sake but he couldn't dig and watch his back at the same time.

Stepping off the porch, he headed for the chicken coop. There was one thing he could do; he would spare her the sight of her son. He kept his eyes on the trees flanking the house and did not look down until he was almost to the spot where the boy had fallen. Then an oath escaped him.

Billy had been dragged off.

Mixed emotions tugged at Fargo. He was glad to be spared the burial. But it would be horrible if a week or a month from now, Devy stumbled on the remains. The image of her partially eaten husband was already seared into her memory. She did not need to see her son in the same grisly state.

The blood trail led off into the trees behind the house. Fargo did not follow it. Wiser, he thought, to wait until Devy and Gwen were up. Should something happen to him while they were asleep, they would be unprotected.

Fargo opted to sit in a chair on the porch rather than go back inside. He had been there a while when he realized he hadn't seen a single buzzard since he found that first dead cow. Usually, carrion brought vultures from miles around. He wondered if the rabies had something to do with it, although, to the best of his recollection, the disease never afflicted birds. Why that should be, he had no idea.

The sun was over an hour high when moving figures appeared out of the haze to the northwest. Fargo was slouched in his chair but instantly shot to his feet. He counted five. Four were on two legs. Strung out in single file, they crossed over a hill and hiked into the valley.

Fargo established they were whites and not Indians when they were still a long way off. Indians moved differently. He also established that the one in the lead had a dog on a leash.

As they came closer, Fargo observed that all four carried rifles and wore a brace of revolvers. They were dressed in homespun and hats with floppy brims. Each was on the stocky side, with a round moon face. They were enough alike to be related.

The man in front was the oldest, his stubble dotted with gray. He had a big belly which bulged over his belt, a powerful chest, and brawny arms. He also wore suspenders. Plodding along at the end of the leash in his left hand was a hound with droopy jowls and long ears. The man's dark, beady eyes regarded Fargo suspiciously as the party came to a stop. "Who the hell are you, mister? And what the hell are you doin' here?"

Fargo resented the man's tone but he reckoned the newcomer was concerned for the Carroways. "You must be Hinkle. I'm a friend of Devy's."

"I'm Leon Hinkle, sure enough, and these are my boys," the man said gruffly. "But I ain't never set eyes on you before. How do I know you're who you say you are and not some varmint who's done Devona harm?"

"You'll see for yourself when she wakes up." Fargo did not like how the sons had fanned out and were looking at their father as if awaiting a signal to start shooting.

"Maybe I'll just have a look-see for my own self," Hinkle declared, and took a step.

Fargo had no real cause to do what he did next, other than he had taken a strong dislike to the man and was angered by Hinkle's overbearing attitude. Leveling the Henry, he said, "That's far enough. She's had a long night and needs her rest."

Hinkle stopped, his beady eyes glued to the Henry's muzzle. A red tinge crept from his thick neck to his hat. Several of his sons brought their rifles to bear but Hinkle gestured sharply. "Any peckerwood who pulls trigger will answer to me. Could be this feller is tellin' the truth."

The son nearest him fidgeted. "But Pa, we came all this way just to see her." Like the rest, he had to be in his twenties.

Spinning around, Leon Hinkle cuffed him, moving so fast the son couldn't dodge if he tried. "How many times must I tell you, Jethro? Don't ever sass me! If there's one thing gets me riled, it's sass."

"Sorry," Pa." Jethro rubbed his cheek. "I just don't understand you sometimes, is all."

"There's a lot you're too dumb to understand. That's why you boys let me do the thinkin' for this family."

Fargo liked Leon Hinkle less and less by the moment. But for the moment he would give him the benefit of the doubt. "Do you happen to know how many families are left besides yours and the Carroways?"

Hinkle leaned on his rifle. "I can't rightly say but it ain't many. Some lit out as soon as the trouble started. Some were taken by hellhounds. Others have come down with rabies." He scratched his stubble. "At the rate things are goin', pretty soon me and my boys will have this whole territory to ourselves." One of the other sons snickered and Hinkle glared at him, then went on. "I'm right surprised to find you here, stranger. Most would have the good sense to fight shy of a rabies outbreak."

The insult wasn't lost on Fargo. "What's your excuse for sticking around?"

"I ain't never run from nothin' in my life," Hinkle boasted. "Folks breed 'em tough where I come from, and I'm the toughest coon there is."

"Until you meet someone tougher."

Hinkle held his rifle so Fargo could see it plainly. An old Sharps, its stock decorated with over a dozen shiny tacks. "You see these? Every one stands for a jackass who made the mistake of thinkin' he was tougher than me. They all learned the hard way that they weren't."

Fargo had met men who carved notches in the grips of their pistols but this was a first. "Afraid you'll forget how many there were?"

Hinkle's face pinched in on itself. "I admire a man who comes right out and says what's on his mind. The problem with that is one day he'll say it to the wrong person and have his wick blown out."

"Mine is still burning." Fargo had made an enemy; he saw it in the hard glint in Hinkle's dark eyes.

Hinkle's hound was straining toward one of the dead hellhounds. Hinkle jerked on the leash and commanded it to sit, which it did. "Looks like you had some excitement here last night."

"If you can call the death of a boy exciting." Fargo had had his full of the man and wished they would all leave.

"Billy Carroway is dead?" Hinkle's tone held little emotion. "Why, ain't that a shame. He was always such a bright one, too. Liked to tease me because he could read and write and I can't. I reckon he doesn't feel so bright now."

It was all Fargo could do to keep himself from punching Hinkle in his moon face. "Be sure and mention that to Devy when she comes down."

"Oh, she knows the boy and me didn't hit it off. But that's the way with kids who have been spoiled. You'd never catch any of my boys treatin' me or any other adult with disrespect. I've taught 'em too well."

"A lot of trips to the woodshed," Fargo guessed, and noticed that one of the boys cast a spiteful glance at the father.

"Spare the rod and spoil the child," Hinkle declared. "Young'uns are like dogs. When they're pups, they need to be whipped regular to keep 'em in line. My pa whipped the tar out of me more times than I can recollect and I turned out fine. All my neighbors in Tennessee thought highly of me."

Fargo sat in the chair with the Henry across his legs. "You're a long way from home."

"Not by choice. I had a little difficulty with a man down to the bank over some money he claimed I hadn't paid. One thing led to another and I had to pack up and head for greener pastures. I'd heard about the Oregon country, how green and pretty it is, but we got this far and decided to stay."

The third son, the youngest, was gaping agog at the front doorway. "Pa! You ain't goin' to believe this!"

"What's that, Toby?"

"There's a horse in that house, Pa. Standin' in there as big as life and swishin' its tail."

"In the house?" The son who had given Hinkle the spiteful look stepped over to look for himself. "I'll be, Pa! Toby is right. There is a horse in there. One of them pintos. Want me to go in and fetch it out for you?"

"Stay right where you're at, Tyrel." For some reason Hinkle seemed disturbed by the discovery. "The horse would be yours, I take it?" he asked Fargo.

Fargo nodded.

"You took it inside so the hellhounds couldn't get at it? Mighty clever. Mighty clever indeed. Our horses were run off by a hellhound the other night and we ain't seen 'em since." Hinkle moved so he could see down the hall. "Fine animal you've got there, mister. I've always wanted me one of them paint horses. I don't suppose you would be willin' to sell it?"

Fargo shook his head.

"I didn't think so. But it never hurts to ask." Then Leon Hinkle said a strange thing. "A man's got to go through the motions. That way his conscience won't bother him later."

The front door opened and out stepped Devona Carroway. She had on the same dress as the night before and had tied a red ribbon in her hair. "Good

61

morning," she said to Fargo, smiling sweetly. "You should have woke me."

Hinkle glanced from her to Fargo and back again. His lips pressed thin and he gave the leash a jerk even though the hound was just sitting there. Clearing his throat, he said, "Sorry to hear about your latest loss, Devona. Truly I am."

"Thank you, Mr. Hinkle."

"Call me Leon, please. If you don't mind my askin', how exactly did the boy die? Did the hellhounds get him?"

"Rabies," Devy said.

"Do tell. We'll both have cause to remember this summer, won't we? You losin' your husband and your boy. Me losin' my wife."

"Mrs. Hinkle is dead?"

Hinkle solemnly nodded. "She came down with rabies and went to her Maker five days ago. It upset me something awful, but when the Good Lord calls us to our reward, we can't hardly say no."

Fargo saw Tyrel give his father another spiteful glance.

"You have my sincere condolences, Mr. Hinkle," Devy was saying. "I know the torment you're going through and it isn't easy to bear."

"That it ain't. My heart has been heavy since we buried her. She and I were together pretty near twenty-five years, and she hardly ever gave me cause to slap her. Can't ask much more of a female." Hinkle smiled. "But like the Bible says, the Lord gives and the Lord takes away. Everything happens for a reason. All we have to do is divine His purpose. It's taken me a while, but I have me an idea why we've lost our spouses."

"There's no purpose to Brian's death that I can see," Devy said. "He was a good husband and a great provider and never harmed a living soul his whole life. He deserved a better death."

"It's darned near blasphemous to question the Almighty's judgement, woman," Hinkle said sternly.

"I prefer Mrs. Carroway," Devy said, equally stern.

"And I'm entitled to question. What sort of God lets things like this happen? Lets innocent people suffer for no earthly reason?"

"You should hear yourself. You're a prime example of why women shouldn't have the right to vote. There's not been a lick of logic in any female ever born." Hinkle chuckled. "That's why men were put on this earth. To set you women straight and show you how things are."

Devy folded her arms. "I don't need to be set straight by you or any other man. I'm a grown woman and I can think as I please."

"Sure you can," Hinkle patronized her. "If it makes you feel better, you go on believin' that."

"There are times, Mr. Hinkle, when you try my patience."

"Be that as it may, you and me now have the same problem and the solution is starin' us right in the face."

"I'm afraid I don't quite follow you," Devy told him.

Fargo did, and he hoped he was wrong. Jethro and Toby were grinning expectantly but Tyrel was frowning.

"Let me spell it out for you, Devona. I've lost my Agnes. You've lost your Brian. We're both alone now. Both with young'uns to look after. Both in need of a mate. If this ain't a case of the Lord givin' and takin', I don't know what is."

"Surely you're not suggesting—?" Devy took a step back. "Why, that's preposterous, Mr. Hinkle."

"What's preposterous about it? Why do you reckon I came all the way over here today?"

"I thought it was to see if we were safe."

Leon Hinkle laughed. "That's only part of it. The main reason I've come is to take you as my new wife."

6

Skye Fargo saw the outburst coming. He saw Devona Carroway stiffen, saw her fists clench and her face flush and her jaw muscles tighten. Leon Hinkle, however, was blind to his blunder. Hinkle was smiling like his announcement was the greatest thing to happen to her since she came into the world. Either the man was dumb as a tree stump or he had no respect for the feelings of others, or both.

"Ponder on it some, woman, and you'll see I'm right. You and me were meant for one another."

"How dare you!" Devy's voice crackled with unleashed emotion. "Agnes is barely cold in her grave and you waltz over here and say you want me to be your wife? Who the hell do you think you are? Marriage isn't like breeding your hounds. You don't pair two people up whether they want to be paired up or not."

Hinkle never lost his smile. "You're takin' this all wrong, Devona. It's the death of your boy. It has you out of sorts. Typical of a woman. Give yourself a week and you'll come around."

Devy stormed off the porch and raised her fists to strike him. "You—you—you!" She could not find a word fitting enough. "You wretched clod! My being a woman has nothing to do with it! I wouldn't be your wife if you were the last man on earth."

Some of Hinkle's confidence faded. "Are you sayin' you won't even consider marryin' me?"

64

"How can I make it any more plain?" Devy jabbed him in the chest. "Very well. Listen closely. I don't find you the least bit attractive. In fact, I find you positively despicable. I saw how you always bossed your poor wife around and never let her get a word in edgewise. She hardly ever smiled, she was so miserable. But you didn't give a damn."

"Now you just hold on," Hinkle began.

"No. *You* hold on." Devy had her hands on her hips. "Did you think I never noticed how you were always looking at me when you thought I wasn't watching? My husband saw it too and wanted to beat you to a pulp but I wouldn't let him. You're a lecher and a pig and I want nothing to do with you from this day on."

Jethro moved toward her. "Hold on, there, woman. No one talks to our pa like that. I ought to slap you silly."

Fargo rose out of the chair and raised the Henry. "That's far enough," he cautioned.

Leon Hinkle was a moon-faced beet, his beady eyes glittering like quartz. He glanced from Devy to Fargo. "It's him, ain't it? You've taken a shine to this stranger and set your sights on him being your man?"

"Get off my property," Devy said.

"You don't want to be doing this," Leon growled. "I don't take kindly to insults. And pretty soon I'm going to be a big man in these parts. Mighty big. You'd be doing yourself a favor by hitchin' your reins to me instead of this meddler."

"I won't tell you again."

Hinkle did not know when to leave well enough alone. "What will you do if we stay? Slap me? My missus did that once and I hit her so hard she couldn't eat solid food for a month. My pa always said women need to be taught their place and I can see you're no exception."

Fargo had listened to all he was going to. "You heard the lady. Take your boys and your hound and skedaddle. And don't pester her again."

65

"What I do ain't for you to say, mister," Hinkle said calmly enough, although he blazed with hate. "My advice to you is to get on that paint of yours and light a shuck before you end up as maggot bait."

Centering the Henry on Hinkle's sternum, Fargo responded, "I'll count to three and then I start shooting."

"You wouldn't dare!" Jethro interjected. He had been growing more and more agitated with each passing moment, and now he let loose with a roar of pure rage and brought up his rifle.

Fargo had been expecting one of them to try something. He was ready, and when Jethro went to shoot, he swivelled and fired. He didn't go for a kill shot. His slug ripped through Jethro's right thigh and Jethro shrieked and dropped.

Toby snatched at a revolver and Fargo instantly covered him. "You'll never clear leather."

Leon Hinkle was quivering with outrage but he did not let it goad him into doing anything rash. "Take your hand off your pistol, boy. This coon's got sand. But there's more than one way to peel a hide, and we're just the ones to teach him."

Jethro had his hands clamped to his wound and was rolling back and forth in the dirt and groaning.

His father walked over and kicked him. "Quit your blubberin'. I taught you better than this. You're not bleedin' that bad. Is the bone broke?"

"I don't think so," Jethro said through clenched teeth.

"Then quit lyin' there like a baby and get up. Toby, Tyrel, come give your brother a hand." Hinkle turned. "Devona, you'll be seein' me again whether you want to or not." He fixed Fargo with a glare. "The same goes for you, mister. We're hill folk and hill folk live for the feud."

The clan departed, Hinkle and the hound bringing up the rear. He glanced back only once, his expression as ripe with menace as that of a riled griz. Fargo kept the

Henry on them until they were stick figures in the distance. When he looked at Devy, tears brimmed her eyes.

"Can you believe his gall? How do people become like that? He has no respect for anyone. No respect for their feelings."

"He's gone," Fargo stressed. "Why fret over it?"

"Because you don't know him like I do. When he sets his mind to something, he doesn't let up until he gets what he wants." Devy placed her palms against her temples and closed her eyes. "I don't need this kind of aggravation. Not now, of all times. Not when I'm all alone with Gwen to look after."

"You're not alone."

Devy hugged him. "Thank you, Skye. It means more than I can say. I've already lost two of those I loved most in the world. It would crush me to lose her as well. I couldn't stand it."

"Lose me how, ma?"

Gwen emerged from the house. Fargo wondered how long she had been standing there, and how much she had overheard. Devy scooped her up and kissed her and acted like nothing had happened.

"Are you hungry, little one? I know I am. Maybe Mr. Fargo will be nice enough to let us have some raisins and crackers for breakfast."

"Help yourselves." Fargo stayed outside until the Hinkles were lost to view over the hills. He had no illusions about what they would try to do. As Hinkle boasted, they were hill folk, and hill folk were notorious feudists. When they made an enemy it was for keeps, and they didn't rest until their enemies were underground, or they were.

Fargo led the Ovaro outside and tied it to the rail. It would need water before another day went by and he knew of only three places to get some; the Snake River, the Palouse River, or the pump behind the stable in Carn. Since the town was a hotbed of rabies and the Palouse River was farther than the Snake, his decision was made for him. He went inside.

Devy and Gwen were at the kitchen table munching on crackers.

"I never knew crackers could taste so good," the girl said. "It would be better if we had jam but we're all out."

"What we need most is water." Fargo looked at Devona when he said it. "We can start for the Snake River whenever you're ready. From there I'll take you on to Fort Bridger."

"I told you last night this is our home and we're not leaving it. I still have a few jars of water in the root cellar. You're welcome to help yourself."

"What happens when you run out?"

"I'll cross that bridge when I come to it." Devy's teeth crunched into a cracker. "Besides, you certainly can't expect me to leave without tending to my son. He needs a proper burial."

"Let me."

"I'm his mother. It's my responsibility."

"One of us should stay with Gwen. She's your responsibility too, so you're elected." Fargo nipped an argument in the bud by going back out.

He was too smart to go blundering into the woods behind the house on foot. Not when the hellhounds that dragged the boy off might be lying low after feasting on the body. He went to the barn for his saddle and saddle blanket and soon had the stallion ready to go. The rest had done it good. It was alert with its head held high as they neared the trees.

Everything was brown, from the grass and the brush to the trees. Leaves hung withered on branches like so many sun-baked prunes. Branches and stems drooped like weary soldiers on parade. Fargo hadn't gone far when he saw the boy's right foot. It had been gnawed off and chewed to the bone. Fifteen yards more and he spotted a severed hand. A terrible stench and a mound of swarming flies pinpointed what was left of young Billy Carroway.

Fargo tied his bandanna around his mouth and nose. He had forgotten to bring a shovel but plenty of fallen branches were handy. It took forty minutes to scoop out a grave. He made it deeper than he had to so the smell wouldn't attract scavengers. To avoid touching the remains, he used a limb to roll the body into the hole. Smaller pieces, like the foot and hand, he flipped and prodded until they fell in. When he was sure he had collected all the body parts there were to be had, he filled in the hole and stamped on the dirt. Afterward, he roved the dry stream bed, gathering the biggest rocks he could find to cover the mound. It would further deter carrion eaters.

By the time Fargo stepped into the stirrups and headed back, almost an hour and a half had gone by. Once again he was pouring sweat, and he could not stop thinking about the water jars in the root cellar.

The front door was wide open. Fargo was sure he had closed it but he figured Devona had opened it to let in air. He stepped onto the porch, and froze. A rifle muzzle was trained on him from inside. Out of the house strode Toby Hinkle. Around the far corner came Tyrel.

"I wish you could see your face, mister," Toby gloated. "Bet you didn't reckon on us gettin' the drop on you like this, did you?"

"Don't try anything and you'll live a while yet," Tyrel said.

Toby snickered. "A short while. Now suppose you unbuckle your belt and let your hardware fall. Real slow-like, unless you're partial to lead poisonin'."

Fargo was mad at himself for being caught flat-footed. "Where are the Carroways?"

"You should be more worried about your own hide," Toby said.

Tyrel stepped onto the porch. "They're with Pa and brother Jethro. I've got to tell you, mister, I've never seen my pa so mad. He could spit nails, he wants you dead so bad. But he wants Mrs. Carroway more, so he took her and left us to surprise you."

"Surprise!" Toby said, and cackled.

As much as it galled him to do as they wanted,

Fargo lowered his gun belt and hiked his hands. "What now?" He kept hoping one of the other would come close enough for him to pounce but they stayed well out of his reach.

"We're goin' for a little walk," Toby declared. "You in front. Head northwest. My brother will bring your pinto."

Fargo grasped at a straw. If he could lure them inside where there wasn't a lot of room to move, maybe he could jump them. "I have food inside. Shouldn't we take it along?"

Toby chuckled. "It's plumb cordial of you to be thinkin' of our stomachs but we've got more vittles than we know what to do with."

"How can that be, with the drought?"

"Our pa plans ahead," Toby said, and laughed.

They headed out, Fargo in front, Toby next, and Tyrel leading the Ovaro. Fargo tried not to think of what Devona must be going through. "Tell me something," he said as they passed the barn. "Do the two of you think your father has the right to take a woman against her will?"

"You don't know much about females," Toby said. "They never know their own minds. I saw that with my ma. She'd say one thing one minute, then after pa explained how things ought to be, she'd change her mind and go along with him. Fickle is what they are."

"Sounds to me like your father browbeat her into doing what he wanted."

"Shows how much you know. Pa didn't beat her more than once a month. She always went along because females can't think as good as men and she knew it. Women need us menfolk to show them how to do things."

Fargo glanced at Tyrel. "You feel that way, too?"

"What's it to you, mister?" Tyrel bristled. "How I feel about things is none of your damn business."

The sun was blistering hot. Fargo did not think he could sweat any more than he already had, but he was wrong. The ankle sheath to his Arkansas Toothpick

70

chafed his skin but he was glad it was there. When the right moment came, he had a surprise in store for the Hinkle boys.

Fargo thought they were headed for Carn but along about the third mile Toby told him to bear more to the north. Presently they came on scores of dead cattle clustered around a dry water hole.

"These belonged to Ed Baxter," Tyrel mentioned. "We offered to take them off his hands but he wouldn't agree to our price of a dollar a head."

"You tried to swindle him," Fargo said.

"We had water, he didn't. We still have water and no one else does. Which is why pretty soon my pa will be the most powerful gent in this part of the territory."

"Hush, damn you," Toby said. "Pa doesn't want us to say anything to anyone, remember?"

"Hell, there's hardly anyone left to say it to," Tyrel replied. "Another month or two and it will all be ours. Pa says in five years we'll be rich. I can hardly wait. I'm so sick of doing without, of always wantin' what others have but I can never afford."

"How does your father plan to get his hands on so much money?" Fargo had a suspicion but he thought it best not to voice it.

"It's the land," Tyrel started to answer.

Toby angrily motioned. "Didn't you hear me? Pa will skin you alive if you keep blabbin'. We can't have anyone catch on until it's too late for us to be stopped, remember?"

"All right. Don't get your britches in a knot."

The sun was a red-hot coal, burning the land and everything in it. Fargo's mouth became so dry it hurt to swallow. His legs grew leaden. But he refused to ask the Hinkles to stop and rest.

Dead cattle were a common sight. Fargo also saw dead deer, several dead rabbits, and a partially devoured coyote. Further on he spied a horse, its rib bones bleached white, and he looked back at the Ovaro, which was plodding along with its head low

71

and its tail drooping. He had to get it water, and he had to do it soon.

To the west buildings shimmered like a desert mirage. It was Carn, tantalizingly close yet so far. Fargo slowed a trifle to see if Toby would say anything, and when he didn't, Fargo slowed even more. Only six feet separated them.

Suddenly Toby halted and looked around. "Over there," he said, pointing at the north slope of a hill they were crossing. "We'll rest a spell."

At the bottom stood a solitary tree, an old oak that somehow had taken root where no other had. The shade it offered wasn't much but Fargo gratefully sank down with his back to the trunk and removed his hat. "How much longer until we're there?"

"Another couple of hours," Tyrel said.

Carn was only an hour away. Fargo bent his legs so his boots were near his right hip, then placed his hat over them. To the Hinkles it appeared perfectly natural.

Tyrel had tied the Ovaro's reins to a low limb and now was hunkered with his head hung low. "I thought Georgia was hot but this beats all. There are times when I wish we never left."

"Pa knows what is best for us," Toby said.

"Sometimes I wonder."

"What's gotten into you lately, Ty? You never talked like this before Ma died. Ever since, you've complained up a storm."

"I've got my reasons," Tyrel said sullenly.

Neither was looking at Fargo. Casually sliding his right hand under his hat, he hitched at his pant leg and slid his finger into his boot. His palm closed around the hilt of the Arkansas Toothpick.

Toby was staring at his brother. "I'd sure like to hear what your reasons are. Pa has noticed how you've been. Yesterday he asked me if I knew why. I told him you missed Ma."

"Don't you miss her?"

"What kind of stupid question is that? Sure I do. I

loved Ma just as much as you or Jethro or Chad or Eli or any of the others."

Fargo eased the Toothpick from his boot.

Tyrel looked up, his expression troubled. "And you never saw fit to question Pa about her death, brother Toby? It never struck you as peculiar, what Pa did?"

"What are you gettin' at? Pa did the only thing he could. As soon as he found out Ma had rabies, he put her out of her misery."

"Strange, isn't it, that Ma never showed any of the symptoms?" Tyrel said. "She couldn't have had it very long."

"Why let her suffer when there wasn't any need? Isn't that what Pa said? He had to do what he did. It's that simple."

With his left hand, Fargo placed his hat on his head, and coiled. His right hand was hidden under his leg.

"I only hope Pa does the same for me if my time comes," Toby was saying. "Rabies is about the worst way there is to die. You can't drink, you can't hardly swallow, and the pain never stops. I'd rather get a bullet through the brain any day. Just like Pa did for our ma."

Fargo's moment had come. He launched himself at them and clipped Tyrel's jaw with a flashing left. A heartbeat later he had the double-edged tip of the toothpick pressed to Toby's jugular. The younger man tried to aim his rifle but turned to granite when Fargo pressed harder. "I'd think twice if I were you."

"Damn you to hell, mister! Pa will tan my hide for this. The last time he took a bullwhip to my back I was laid up for a month."

Fargo relieved Toby of the rifle and tossed it into the brown grass. He also reclaimed his gun belt, which Toby had buckled and slung over a shoulder. As he cocked the Colt, Tyrel sat up, rubbing his chin. "I should shoot you both."

"What's stoppin' you?" Toby blustered.

Common sense urged Fargo to do it. But he wasn't a cold-blooded killer, and the Hinkles hadn't harmed him. Threatened to, yes, but he wouldn't gun them down for spewing hot air. This time.

"You're a tricky varmint, you know that?" Toby grumbled. "Where did you have that pigsticker hid, anyhow?"

"Wouldn't you like to know?" Fargo yanked him to his feet, relieved him of his other weapons, and shoved him against the tree. "Stand there and don't move." He pointed the Colt at Tyrel. "Your turn. We can do this easy or we can do it hard. Which will it be?"

Tyrel chose to undo his own gun belt and to carefully drop it and his knife next to his rifle. Arms elevated, he stepped next to his brother. "You're fixin' to go after her, aren't you?"

Fargo didn't bother to answer. Of course he was going after her. She was a friend and even if she weren't, there was the little girl. He couldn't turn his back on them and still look at himself in the mirror. "Start walking."

Toby had touched a finger to a tiny cut on his neck and was licking a drop a blood from the fingertip. "You're lettin' us live? You must have less sand than Pa figured."

"Be quiet," Tyrel said.

His brother refused to heed. "Wait until Pa hears how soft you are, mister. He'll laugh himself silly. The least you should have done is make it so we can't reach home before you get there."

"Good advice," Fargo said, and shot him in the thigh.

Collapsing in agony, Toby screeched and blubbered and cursed a torrent. He was as rabid as a man could be without actually being rabid.

"Pick him up and get going," he directed Tyrel.

"Can't I bandage him first? He could bleed to death before we reach home."

"Then you better walk fast."

It took them a while to hobble over the hill. Once they were gone, Fargo wasted no time in mounting up

74

and heading for town. The stallion needed water before he went after Devy and Gwen. It would only be a brief delay. He could still reach the Hinkle farm before Tyrel and Toby.

The stable sat slightly apart from the other buildings. Fargo hoped that by coming up on it from the rear and keeping it between him and the others, his arrival would go unnoticed. He wanted to sneak in and get out again without any trouble.

As usual, the town was deceptively tranquil. A feeling came over Fargo, a sense that unseen eyes were on him, but only one window overlooked the pump and its curtains were drawn. He reined in at the corral, tied the Ovaro, and hurried to the front of the stable. The doors were wide open, as he had left them, and the bucket was where he had dropped it.

Fargo was bending to grip the handle when he heard a sound from down the street. It was a sound he thought he should know but couldn't quite place it. As he moved to the doorway it was repeated. Louder this time, and closer. He stepped into the shadows so he wouldn't be seen.

Out of the general store shuffled Pete Spence, the rabid barber, his mouth white with foamy spit. In his hands was a long length of chain which he shook as he walked.

It was the rattling Fargo had heard. He stayed where he was, expecting Spence to go into another building or wander off. Instead, the crazed barber came directly toward the stable.

7

Skye Fargo backed deeper into the shadows. He wanted to avoid using the Colt if he could help it. A gunshot might attract unwanted attention from others like Spence, or hellhounds in the vicinity.

Rabies had the barber well in its grip. Wild-eyed and drooling, he moved in stiff-legged fashion, his body constantly subject to jerks and twitches. He swung the chain from side to side, flailing empty air. Step by lumbering step he came to the doorway, then halted and peered at the stalls. Gurgling, he shambled inside.

Fargo could slip out undetected but he was curious to learn what the madman was up to. He soon found out.

The barber shambled to the stall containing the stableman's body. Grinning hideously, he beat it with the chain, swinging over and over and over, attacking it as if it were alive.

Fargo slid along the wall and was almost to the door when he heard footsteps. He ducked back into the shadows just in time. Into the stable shuffled another rabies-afflicted travesty of humanity—an older man more ravaged by the disease than Spence. Growling and grunting, he stalked toward the unsuspecting barber, who was so engrossed in beating the body that the second madman was on top of him before he realized he was not alone. Spence snarled and tried to turn but the other man lunged and they grappled, biting and snapping like hellhounds as they fell to the ground.

Fargo had seen enough. He slipped outside and jogged to the rear of the stable. The Ovaro was patiently waiting. Placing the bucket next to the pump, Fargo worked the handle. It creaked like a rusty hinge. He pumped for minutes before water appeared, trickling from the spout in droplets. Gradually the trickle increased to a steady if meager flow. He had to pump furiously to maintain it.

The bucket filled much too slowly. Fargo glanced at the Ovaro and saw the stallion gaze past him. He whirled a fraction of a heartbeat before the end of the barber's chain missed his head by a finger's-width. Letting go of the pump, he skipped out of reach.

The barber lurched after him. In addition to the drool glistening on the man's chin, blood now dampened his throat and chest. Whole chunks had been ripped from his neck, and pink flesh hung in loose folds. His left ear had been bitten off, his left cheek was half gone. He swung the chain again but it fell short.

Fargo drew the Colt. He did not have time to waste. Every minute he delayed was another minute Devona and Gwen spent as Leon Hinkle's captives. Thumbing back the hammer, he shot the barber between the eyes.

Again Fargo worked the pump handle. He thought to glance toward the street and saw the older madman staggering toward him. Before the man could come any closer, Fargo pitched him into eternity with a slug through the heart.

During the next several minutes the water stopped flowing twice. Fargo suspected the well was on the verge of going dry like all the others. The bucket was three-fourths full when a voice slashed at him from the corral.

"Keep your hands on the pump and you'll live."

A townsman had the barrel of a Spencer resting on

77

the top rail, centered on Fargo. He was middle-aged, with pudgy cheeks and a broad nose. "I don't want the water," he said.

"Then quit pointing that thing at me." Fargo did not stop working the lever. He was thinking of Devy.

"Sorry I can't oblige. You see, it's your horse I'm after." The man climbed to the top rail and swung a leg over.

"I can't let you have him," Fargo said.

"You can't stop me." The townsman was scared and trying hard not to let it show. "I don't want to kill you but I will if you force me. I'm tired of hiding out in my cellar." He lowered his other leg. "I saw you yesterday but wasn't about to come out with those stinking hellhounds skulking about."

"I can't let you have him," Fargo repeated.

"Blame yourself, not me. Why in hell do you keep hanging around? You never should have come back." He had one foot on the ground. "Be thankful I'm letting you live."

Fargo wasn't thankful. He was mad. Mad clean through. Stealing a horse was considered the worse offense on the frontier. Worse than robbery. Worse than murder. Horse thieves were strung up without benefit of a trial. The man had to know that.

"You're probably wondering why I didn't leave weeks ago," the would-be thief said. "I was scared, mostly. Scared of the hellhounds, and scared of coming down with rabies." He took a step toward the pinto. "Have you ever been scared, mister?"

Fargo just stared.

"I can't help it I'm short on courage. I've always been that way. I've never shot anyone in my life, but I swear to God I'll shoot you if you try to stop me."

"It's not too late," Fargo tried a final time. "Put the rifle down and I'm willing to forget this and do what I can to help you."

"I can't. This could be the last chance I'll have to get shed of this place." He reached out to undo the reins. "I'm heading west. I'll leave your horse at the first settlement I come to."

Fargo slid his hands lower on the pump handle and turned so his holster brushed the pump.

"I hope you won't hold this against me. But in a situation like this, it's every person for themselves." The man had the reins almost off. "Never stole a horse before. I guess there's a first time for everything."

"There's also a last time."

Just then the stallion nickered and stomped a front hoof, and the man glanced at it.

Fargo had no need to aim. At that range, he snapped off a shot from the hip, and his countless hours of practice paid off.

It took another ten minutes to finish filling the bucket. The whole while, Fargo watched the street and the far side of the stable. No one else appeared. He gave the Ovaro enough water to tide it over a spell, filled his canteen, then cupped his hands in the bucket and slaked his own thirst.

The Hinkle farm was supposed to lie due north of Carn but Fargo was unsure how far. To spare the Ovaro he held to a walk. He saw a lot of cow tracks and a lot of dead cows. He saw a lot of hellhound tracks, too, but no dead hellhounds. He hadn't gone far when his throat was as dry as it had been before his visit to the pump, but he didn't touch the canteen. He was saving it for when he had Devy and Gwen.

The Hinkles had chosen a flat-topped hill for their homestead. It consisted of a house, a long, low shed, a few smaller outbuildings, and a corral that, at the moment, was empty. Fargo could not tell much else from the crown of a thicket-covered hill a quarter of a mile away. It was as close as he dared venture until nightfall. He saw a lot of people and dogs moving about.

Fargo hoped Hinkle left Devona alone. She had been through enough hardship and heartache without having him force himself on her.

Sunset was hours away. Fargo lay on his stomach

on the hot ground with his chin on his forearms, and dozed. He roused himself every now and again to scour the nearby hills for hellhounds, Hinkles and rabid animals.

At about four o'clock, by the position of the sun, a pair of figures materialized to the southeast. One was leaning on the other. Tyrel and Toby started shouting as soon as they came within sight of the house, and it wasn't long before several of their kin hurried out to meet them. The two had made better time than Fargo counted on.

He wondered how many Hinkles there were. He'd only met four. But Toby had mentioned a "Chad" and an "Eli" and "others."

Shortly before sunset, howls echoed across the hills. Fargo woke up and raised his head. It came from the long shed. From the sound of things, the Hinkles had an army of bloodhounds. Hounds that could track anything, anywhere. Fargo reminded himself he would do well to keep that in mind.

Twilight took forever descending. Fargo stayed put until it succumbed to a canopy of stars. Then he rose, swung onto the pinto, and circled to approach the flat-topped hill from the west. The night brought with it the eerily ululating cries of hellhounds from all points of the compass. Five or six packs were roaming the countryside. When they howled, so did the hounds in the long shed.

Fargo was only a few hundred yards from the base of the flat-topped hill when he spied the red glow of a cigarette midway up the north side. A lookout, he thought as he dismounted. He did not like leaving the Ovaro but he could not get close enough on horseback to take the lookout by surprise. Removing his spurs, he placed them in his saddlebags.

The glow grew brighter as Fargo cat-footed up the slope. Suddenly it seemed to wink out. He stopped in case the lookout had spotted him, but when no shots rang out and there was no outcry, he went on. The dot winked on and off again, and soon he discovered why.

The man smoking the cigarette was pacing back and forth in the middle of a stand of trees.

It was an unusual spot for a lookout, Fargo thought, until a match flared and another man, seated on an old crate near a small shed, lit a lantern. The two had the stocky bodies and moon faces typical of Hinkles. They began talking. Fargo crabbed to a tree within earshot, and hunkered.

"Did you see her?" the one with the cigarette was asking. "Isn't she just about the prettiest filly you ever did see?"

"Pa sure didn't waste any time findin' someone new," said the man on the crate. "Ma must be turnin' over in her grave."

"You're just upset because you were always Ma's favorite," the smoker responded. "But I reckon that's natural, brother Clyde, you bein' the oldest and all."

"It's too soon, Arvil."

"Pa doesn't think so and that's all that counts." Arvil took a drag on his cigarette.

"What I want to know is when he's goin' to let *us* take a bride," Clyde said bitterly. "I'm twenty-eight, damn it. I'm entitled to a woman of my own."

"Pa says he didn't get hitched until he was thirty and what was good enough for him is good enough for us."

"Arvil, you're twenty-six. Plenty old enough to get hitched. But did Pa let you marry that gal from the wagon train you cottoned to last year? He did not."

"She was only fourteen. Pa thought that was too young for me."

"Hell," Clyde spat. "Back home cousin Jack married cousin Bonnie and she was only eleven. I didn't hear Pa complain then."

"Maybe we should talk to him. Explain that we're grown men and grown men have needs. He has them too. He said that's part of the reason he wants this Carroway woman so bad."

Fargo edged forward. He glanced down to spot dry twigs or downed limbs and discovered an astounding fact; the grass was green. Green and soft and thick as wool. For it to be so lush there had to be water present, and a lot of it. He studied the shed with renewed interest. It was almost as wide as it was tall, and a padlock hung on the door.

Clyde had his chin in his hands. "I doubt Pa will let either of us find a female until after this whole business is done with. And then he'll likely cook up another excuse for us not to marry."

Arvil agreed, adding, "The only bright spot in this whole mess is that we're going to have more land than we know what to do with."

"Pa will, anyway," Clyde said.

Fargo noticed that the leaves on the branches bathed in the glow of the lantern were as green as the grass. So was a bush beside the shed.

Arvil blew a smoke ring into the air. "I wish to hell those stupid hounds hadn't scared our horses off. Pa should learn how to control them better."

"The horses will stray on back eventually." Clyde patted the shed. "We've got the only water for miles around and they know it."

A few more feet and Fargo was where he wanted to be. He stood up, the Henry to his shoulder. "Touch your pistols and you die."

Dumfounded, the pair stayed glued in place as Fargo stepped from the trees. "Where does your father have the woman and the girl?"

Arvil found his voice first. "Up in the house."

"Where *exactly*?" Fargo's best bet was to get in, grab the Carroways, and get out before the alarm was spread.

"In our ma's old bedroom. It's on the east side of the house."

Clyde slowly rose. "Shut up, Arvil. Don't you recognize this varmint from what the others told us? He's the one who shot Jethro and Toby."

"Sure I recognize him," Arvil said, "and I don't want him to shoot me."

"Unlock the padlock," Fargo directed. He planned to lock them inside.

"We can't," Arvil said. "Our pa has the only key. He doesn't trust us not to help ourselves to some water when he's not around."

Fargo believed him. It would be just like Leon Hinkle not to trust his own sons. "It's a spring, isn't it?" There was no other explanation for the green grass and green trees. The Hinkles had a spring that never dried up. An unending supply of water, enough to help their neighbors and the people in town, but they had been unwilling to share.

Arvil bobbed his chin. "One of our hounds found it when we were scoutin' around for land to settle."

Clyde shifted his weight from one foot to the other. "We don't take kindly to havin' our kin shot, mister. Hurt one of us and you have the rest to deal with."

It would be pointless for Fargo to try to justify what he had done. The blood bond the brothers shared was unbreakable. They would take revenge on anyone who harmed one of their own. Any moment now, Clyde would unlimber his revolver. Fargo couldn't let that happen.

"Back my play," Clyde said to Arvil. "He can't get both of us."

Fargo was on them before either could blink. He smashed the Henry's stock against Clyde's jaw, spun, and slammed Arvil across the temple. They crumpled like a house of cards. He threw their six-guns into the undergrowth, then brought the Ovaro up the hill. Taking the rope from his saddle, he bound them, hand and foot. He cut strips from their shirts for gags.

Fargo wanted to see the spring for himself. The shed was not well constructed. Gaps between the planks were wide enough for him to stick his fingers through. He braced his right foot against one, bunched his shoulders, and pulled on the one beside it. With a squeak the nails gave way. He removed two more planks the same way, making an opening wide enough for him to squeeze through. The water smell was strong and sweet.

The spring took up nearly the entire shed. Squatting, he tasted it. The water was delicious. That a rogue like Leon Hinkle should possess such bounty while the farms of those around him withered to dust was an injustice screaming to be remedied.

Fargo squeezed out of the shed. He removed more planks, enough so the Ovaro could stick its head in and drink if it wanted. Then he climbed to the crest and flattened. The Hinkle farm was lit up like a New Orleans whorehouse. Light shone from every window and a lantern hung on the front porch. Off among the hills a hellhound howled and was answered by a hound in the long shed. Shortly thereafter a Hinkle came out of the shed and walked into the house. Fargo moved to where he could see in several windows.

At a kitchen table sat Tyrel, Toby and Jethro, eating. In another room two others were playing cards. Fargo did not see Leon. Odds were, the family patriarch was with Devona. The thought spurred him into hurrying around to the east. A window was lit but the curtains had been pulled.

Fargo had not seen any lookouts. It troubled him. Leon Hinkle knew he would come for the Carroways. So why hadn't Hinkle arranged a leaden reception? He shoved the thought to the back of his mind, slipped soundlessly to the house, and crouched below the sill. The window had been propped open about halfway and he could hear those inside. Devy was talking.

"—will never agree. You can starve me. You can beat me. But I will never, ever become your wife."

"Oh really?" Leon Hinkle said. "And what about that sweet little gal curled up on the bed asleep? Seems to me you should be thinkin' as much of her welfare as your own."

"You would threaten a child? Is there no limit to how low you'll stoop?"

"Don't put words in my mouth, woman. All I'm sayin' is that it would be to her benefit as much as yours to be part of this family. Pretty soon now we're goin' to be rich and powerful."

"So you keep bragging. I'll believe it when pigs fly."

"If you only knew. I have a secret or two, Devona. Secrets that will amaze the daylights out of you. I'm not the dumb hick you think I am. I never was. I settled here for a purpose and I've been workin' hard ever since toward makin' myself king of the territory. It's all about to pay off."

Devy's laugh was laced with scorn. "King of a country of the dead is no king at all."

"It won't always be dead. The drought will end. The rabies will end. By then the town and all the land around it for as far as you can see will be mine. Think about that."

"You're forgetting the hellhounds. What good will it do to own all the land if your cattle are butchered and you can't go anywhere without being attacked?"

Now it was Hinkle who laughed. "The hellhounds won't be around forever. Mark my words." A door latch scraped. "I'll let you get your rest. But be warned. Tryin' to escape is pointless. There are hellhounds everywhere. You wouldn't want them to do to you and your girl what they did to that uppity husband of yours."

"What do you mean by uppity?" Devy asked, but she received no answer.

Fargo heard the door close. He parted the curtains and saw Gwen at the head of the bed, asleep, her thumb in her mouth. Devy was at the foot of the bed with her head hung in despair. Easing over the sill, he placed a hand on her shoulder. She nearly jumped out of her skin. For a moment he thought she would cry out but she caught herself and threw her arms around him.

"Skye!" she whispered. "Oh, Skye!"

"I'm getting you out of here."

Devy began to cry. "You shouldn't have come. A

85

while ago Hinkle told me he was hoping you would try to rescue us. He said he has a special surprise in store for you. His very words."

"Let me worry about him. Grab Gwen and we'll light a shuck. My horse isn't far." Fargo stooped and looked out the window. None of Hinkle's boys were anywhere around. "Hurry."

Gwen stirred and mumbled when Devy lifted her, but did not wake up. Fargo slid out first, leaned the Henry against the house, and took Gwen so Devy could climb out, then gave her back. In the distance hellhounds were howling. As usual, the hounds in the shed replied in kind.

Fargo guided Devona through the dark to the slope overlooking the spring. They descended quickly, Devy with Gwen draped over a shoulder. Fargo came last in case someone tried to stop them.

The trees were a welcome haven. Devona reached the center first. "Is this where your horse is supposed to be?"

Fargo had been watching behind them. He whirled and received two shocks. The first was that the Ovaro was gone. The second, so were Clyde and Arvil. Their father hadn't lied to Devy. A trap *had* been set, and now its jaws were closing. "Run," he said.

They reached the lower edge of the trees and were brought to a stop by a series of howls from lower down. Hellhounds were coming up the slope toward them.

"This way," Fargo said, and ran north. No sooner did they step from the stand than more howls pierced the night, and more hellhounds appeared.

Gwen woke up and blinked in confusion. "What's going on, Ma? Where are we? How did we get outside?"

"Hush, sweetheart." Devona put her down and gripped her hand. "Stay by me, do you understand? Never let go."

Tugging on Devona's dress, Fargo pointed to the south. It was the only way. By now the Hinkles were bound to have heard the howls and the hilltop would be swarming with them.

Fear goaded Devona and Gwen into crashing through the brush like a pair of frightened deer. Fargo was only a step behind. They broke from cover on the south side of the stand and were met by another chorus of feral howls. Fargo swore. The hellhounds had them surrounded on three sides.

"What do we do?" Devy beseeched him.

There was only one thing to do. "Into the clearing," Fargo said, and backpedaled, covering their retreat as more hellish shapes flitted through the night toward them. They reached the center of the stand and had nowhere else to go.

Hellhounds were converging from the north, east and south, dozens howling at once. A bestial legion with a craving for human flesh, and they had chosen Fargo and the Carroways as their meal.

"I'm scared, Ma!" Gwen wailed. She was clinging to her mother in frantic desperation.

"Everything will be all right," Devy lied.

Fargo saw pinpoints of light in the vegetation. But these were not cigarettes. They were eyes. The eyes of hellhounds, reflecting the gleam of the lantern. Scores of hellhounds, shoulder to hairy shoulder, their ears laid back, their fangs bristling. Far too many for him to down them all.

"Into the shed!" Fargo cried, and pushed Devona and Gwen toward the opening he had made. It was their last resort, and it would not keep the hellhounds out for long. "Go! Go!"

Gwen scrambled through and reached out for her mother. Devy followed and turned. "You too."

Fargo planted himself in front of the opening and faced the hybrids. He was surprised they hadn't rushed him yet. A big one to the left was slightly in front and might be the leader. Fargo sighted on him and waited for the beast to coil.

Then the world went mad.

Out of the darkness behind the hellhounds strode a stocky figure with a moon face. Laughing lustily, he waded into their bestial ranks, and they parted to let him pass. Not one growled. Not one tried to bite him.

"What's the matter, big man?" Leon Hinkle smirked. "Hellhound got your tongue?"

8

It took a lot to shock Fargo. To shock him to where he was at a loss for words. To where he could only stare in complete bewilderment as the source of his shock mocked him with gruff laughter.

"I suggest you lower the rifle," Leon Hinkle said. "All I need do is snap my fingers and you'll be torn to pieces." He raised his hand with his thumb against his fingers, ready to do just that.

The hellhounds were primed to attack. Their bodies taut, they growled and snapped, bloodlust gleaming in their eyes.

Fargo lowered the Henry.

Beyond the hybrids other Hinkles appeared. The hellhounds did not turn and attack. They did not even look at them. The hellhounds were watching Leon Hinkle, their lord and master, awaiting his command.

"I wish you could have seen your face just now," Leon said. "It was downright hilarious." He grinned from ear to ear. "Can't tell you how much I've been lookin' forward to this. You have a lot comin' to you for what you did to my boys and for tryin' to steal my woman out from under me."

From the shed came Devona's angry, "I am not your woman, damn you!"

Leon gazed at the opening. "Now, now, my dear. That's not fit language for a lady. Come on out. And bring the child. Have no fear. My pets won't harm you so long as I'm around."

Fargo's shock had finally worn off. "Your pets?"

"Yes, indeed." Leon placed his hand on the head of the biggest hellhound and the animal nuzzled his leg as would a tame dog. "I'll make it all clear to you soon enough." He took the Henry. "You might be wonderin' why I don't kill you outright. But where's the fun in that?"

Leon gestured and the pack parted. Tyrel and Clyde and Arvil came through, and while Clyde and Arvil covered Fargo with revolvers, Leon handed the Henry and Fargo's gun belt and Colt to Tyrel.

"My boys aim to have some fun with you, too. Jethro and Toby in particular. They can't wait to show you how they liked bein' shot."

"Leave him alone," Devona said, still inside the shed.

Leon turned. "Damn it. Didn't I tell you to come out of there?" When she did not respond, he said, "Why are women so pigheaded? What do you hope to accomplish? If you're not out here in ten seconds, I'll have my boys drag you and your girl out by the hair. So help me God."

Holding Gwen close, Devona eased on through and stood trembling with anger. "I wish I had a gun. I'd shoot you, and hang the consequences."

"I believe you would," Hinkle said gleefully. "That's a good sign. I like a gal with spunk. My Agnes, she used to have it, but she lost it as the years wore on."

"I will never be your wife," Devona flatly declared.

"Agnes felt that way when we first met but I taught her how to think right and do my biddin'." Leon smiled at the hellhounds. "Just as I've taught them to do my biddin'. I've always had a knack for teachin' things how to behave."

"Bending them to your will is more like it."

"Call it what you want." Leon shrugged. "The results are the same and that's all that matters." He paused. "Now then. Suppose we go on up?" He grinned at Fargo. "Need I remind you not to lift a finger against me or mine?"

Fargo yearned to wipe that smirk off Hinkle's face. But the hellhounds would be on him at the first blow, and he couldn't do the Carroways any good if he were dead. He had to stay alive as long as he could in the hope the Hinkles would make a mistake and he could spirit Devy and Gwen out of there.

At a command from their master, the hellhounds formed a bristling phalanx. Leon was enormously pleased with himself, and as they hiked toward the house, he crowed, "Yes, sir. Everything is comin' together just like I planned. And a lot sooner, too. The drought and the rabies helped."

"You're insane," Devona said.

"On the contrary, woman. I've had this planned for years. Ever since one of my hounds mated with a coyote and gave me a litter of these beauties." Leon patted the big hybrid. "They're snake mean. But if you train 'em from the day they open their eyes, they're not much different than a dog."

They came to the top and crossed toward the house. Suddenly Devy stopped. She looked like a bolt of lightning had struck her. "Wait a minute. You've been behind the hellhounds all along? That means—" She stopped, aghast.

Leon Hinkle did not know when to keep his mouth shut. "The truth has finally sunk in, has it? Yes, I sicced my hellhounds on your precious Brian. And I must say, it was a pleasure watchin' 'em rip him apart."

Devy shrieked like an alley cat and hurled herself at Hinkle. Fargo tried to grab her but she sidestepped. Her nails raked Leon's face, leaving bloody furrows in their wake. She tried to gouge out his eyes but Leon seized her by the wrists. The next second, two of his sons pinned her arms.

Fargo was worried about the hellhounds attacking but all they did was growl. He caught hold of Gwen as she started to go to her mother's aid.

Touching a hand to his bloody cheek, Leon balled his fist to hit Devy but didn't. "No. Not here. Not now. I'll teach you, sure enough. But I'll do it good and proper so you learn never to lay a hand on me again." Spinning on his heels, he stomped inside.

The house was as slovenly as its owners. Dirty pots and pans were heaped high on the kitchen counter and bits and pieces of food dotted the floor. Down a hall and to the left was the parlor, as much a mess as the kitchen.

Leon had regained some of his composure. "You'll have to excuse how the place looks," he said to Devy. "Without Agnes here to nag us, we don't keep it as clean as we should."

Any immediate hopes Fargo had of escaping were dashed when several of the sons ushered him at gunpoint into a windowless room. They were about to close the door when Tyrel said, "Hold it." Squatting, Tyrel lifted Fargo's right pant leg, revealing the ankle sheath. "You didn't think I'd forget this pigsticker of yours, did you? Not after you nearly slit my throat with it?"

Into the room hobbled Jethro Hinkle, using an old broom as a crutch. His right thigh had been bandaged and the bandage was stained with blood. "I was hopin' I'd see you again." He started to draw his revolver.

Tyrel moved between them. "Don't even think it. Pa says we're not to touch him yet."

"Why the hell not? He shot me!" Jethro put his hand on his brother as if to shove him out of the way.

"He also shot Toby," Tyrel reminded him, then stepped to one side. "But if you want to buck Pa, go right ahead."

Muttering, Jethro hobbled back out into the hall. "I

can wait. Just so Pa lets me get my licks in. I want to hear this polecat beg for his life before I'm done."

"You'll have a long wait," Fargo told him.

They slammed the door and locked it.

A small dresser sat in a corner. Fargo went through each of its drawers in search of a weapon but all the drawers contained were clothes. In the other corner was a chair, against the back wall a bed. Dropping onto the floor, he wriggled underneath it. Some beds had wire bottoms and wire made a great garrote; this one had wooden slats.

There was nothing for it, then, but to wait for the Hinkles to make the next move. Fargo lay on the bed and pulled his hat brim over his eyes. He imagined they wouldn't keep him waiting long and he was right. Inside of half an hour the door was thrown open and Clyde and Arvil stalked in, their pistols drawn.

"On your feet," Clyde ordered. "Don't ask me why, but Pa has decided we're goin' to feed you before we kill you."

Mealtimes were an occasion for the entire clan to gather in a room off the kitchen. Leon Hinkle sat at the head of a long table. On his right were Devy and Gwen, on his left an empty chair. All the boys were there, nine all told. So were a couple of hounds, lying behind Leon's chair.

Everyone had fallen silent when Fargo entered. Jethro and Toby were across the table from him, Jethro holding his fork like he wanted to bury it in Fargo's face.

Leon smiled grandly. "Now that we're all here we can begin." Folding his hands, he said grace, ending with, "And bless us, Lord, me and my boys, and help us to make our dream come true."

Devy snorted. "Listen to you! As if the Almighty stoops to helping murdering scum."

With the speed of a striking rattler, Leon slapped her across the cheek. "Watch your mouth, woman.

I've put up with all the guff I'm going to take. Especially about the Almighty."

"Leave my ma alone!" Gwen cried. "You're a mean, awful man, and I hope something terrible happens to you."

Leon jabbed a thick finger in her face. "What goes for the goose goes for the goslin'. Keep a civil tongue in that mouth of yours, girl, or I'll have it washed out with lye soap."

"Lay a hand on my daughter and I'll kill you," Devy vowed.

Fargo wouldn't put it past Hinkle to hit her again. To divert Leon's attention he commented, "You're real good at scaring women and children. How are you when it comes to a man?"

Leon leaned back. "I've killed my share, as my boys will testify. And I've got a special death planned for you. I can't say what it is right now 'cause I don't want to spoil the surprise." He glanced at Clyde. "What are you standin' there for? Shouldn't you and Arvil be fetchin' the food?"

"It's not our turn, Pa," Arvil said.

"You'll do it when I say to, and I am damn well sayin' to." Leon clucked in disapproval as they hurried into the kitchen. "I swear, the older young'uns get, the worse they get."

Devy had not been cowed by the slap. "I don't want to hear about your hellions. I want to hear about the hellhounds. About how you sent them after my Brian and murdered him."

"He was a special case. Mostly I let 'em roam as they want. They always come back eventually." Leon smiled. "All the time I was pretendin' to hunt 'em, I was doin' no such thing. I wanted 'em to terrorize folks. I wanted people to give up their farms and leave so I could lay claim to the properties myself."

The scheme was clever, Fargo had to admit. No one would think to link the Hinkles to the hellhounds. The drought and the rabies outbreak had worked in their favor by forcing more people out that much sooner.

Leon had gone on. "There will come a time when they'll outlive their usefulness and I'll have to dispose of 'em. I can't have 'em attackin' the cattle I'll be bringin' in, after all."

"Or your horses?" Fargo asked, remembering a comment Hinkle made at the Carroway farm.

"That could have been avoided. My boys know some of the hellhounds are wilder than others. I told 'em time and time again to keep an eye on the horses when hellhounds are runnin' loose near the corral. But one got in with the horses and spooked 'em. They broke through the fence and ran off. That was a week ago and we ain't seen hide nor hair of 'em since."

Clyde and Arvil returned bearing wooden trays heaped high with food; slabs of beef, slices of venison, potatoes, loaves of bread and a bowl of butter, gravy made from flour and water, and more.

Fargo did not let the current state of affairs spoil his appetite. He needed to keep his strength up. Devy and Gwen, though, only helped themselves to small pieces of meat which they barely touched.

The Hinkles were not much for table talk while they were eating. They were too busy stuffing food into their mouths and chomping with their mouths open. Leon did not say another word until he pushed his plate back, belched, and contentedly patted his belly. "Not bad. It don't compare to my wife's cookin' but she was a wizard at the stove." He gazed at Devy. "I hope you can cook half as good as she could."

"I won't be around long enough for you to find out."

"Think so, do you? The sooner you accept the fact you and me will be man and wife, the more peace of mind you'll have." Leon pushed his chair back and rose. "Now then, suppose I show you somethin' no one outside my kin has ever laid eyes on."

Hinkle was referring to the long, low shed. With seven of his sons in tow, their weapons on Fargo, they crossed from the house. Leon lit a lantern hanging on a peg, raised it over his head, and opened the shed door. "After you."

Fargo had an inkling what they would see. Cages were lined up from end to end, wall to wall. Hunting hounds were in a few near the door. Hellhounds were in all the rest. Hellhounds pacing, hellhounds scratching, hellhounds with litters. The cages had not been cleaned in ages and the stink was abominable.

"We keep about half here at any one time," Leon said, leading them to a cage with a female and nine pups. "As it is, we have almost more than we can handle."

"Aren't you afraid they'll turn on you?" Fargo asked.

"Oh, some act up now and then, but we shoot 'em dead. Raisin' these critters is like playin' with fire and I don't intend to be burnt." Hinkle walked to the far end and showed them a small hanging door on hinges. "This is how they get in when there ain't no one around. We teach 'em to use it from the day they can walk."

"How did you keep all this from your neighbors?" Fargo was stalling on the off chance one of the Hinkles would let down his guard and he could get his hands on a revolver.

"We never cottoned much to visitors so they left us pretty much alone. The few who couldn't take the hint never took a gander in here. We told 'em it was our hound kennel."

"It should be burned to the ground with these vile creatures in it," Devy declared.

"In time it will be," Leon said, and winked.

They headed for the door. Arvil was watching the puppies, his revolver loose in his hand, the barrel pointed down.

Fargo tensed to lunge. He would grab the Remington, jam the barrel against Leon's temple, and tell the others to drop their six-guns. Then it was on to the corral, where the Hinkles had put the Ovaro. Once in the saddle, he would ride like the wind, and as soon as the Carroways were out of danger, he would show the Hinkles it had been a mistake to ever leave Georgia.

Suddenly a gun muzzle was jammed hard against Fargo's ribs. "Don't even think it," Clyde sneered. "I saw how you were lookin' at him."

Leon hung the lantern on the peg and they went out. Jethro and Toby were waiting on the porch, propped on their crutches.

"How about your promise, Pa?" Jethro asked. "Do we get to wallop the tar out of him? We promise not to get carried away."

Toby shook a fist. "Ten minutes, Pa. That's all we want for what he did to us. Ten minutes."

"Just so you don't kill him," Leon said. "It might do my future wife and her brat to watch so they know what's in store for 'em if they don't start behavin'."

Fargo resisted but he was outnumbered. Four Hinkles held his arms in vise-like grips and twisted his arms behind a porch post, and two others bound him. Devy tried to push through them but he looked at her and shook his head. "Not on my account."

"How touchin'," Leon scoffed. He had plopped down on a bench. "We'll see if she still has a hankerin' for you after my boys get done."

Jethro gave his crutch to Tyrel, limped to the post, and set himself. "You're goin' to be sore as hell in the mornin', I can guarantee."

The first eight or nine punches were agony. After that it wasn't quite so bad. Fargo grit his teeth and bore the waves of pain that washed over him. His chest and sides bore the worst. For some reason Tyrel didn't hit his face. Nor did Toby when it was his turn.

Fargo wasn't sure how long they beat him. He lost consciousness for a while and when he opened his eyes again he was being carried down the hall and into the room they put him in before. He landed on the bed with a *thump* and someone threw his hat at him and said something that made the others laugh.

My turn will come, Fargo thought, and sank into a deep, dreamless sleep. When he woke up he could barely move, it hurt so much. He sat up, shoved his hat onto his head, and leaned against the wall. The house was quiet. It must be the middle of the night. Fargo stood up. He swayed like a drunk but it wasn't from rotgut. His ribs screamed at him with every step he took. He tried the latch in the hope they had forgotten to lock the door, but they hadn't forgotten.

Fargo sprawled out on the bed. Whatever else they had in store would not take place until morning. He might as well make the best of it and get more rest. Sleep proved elusive. He was too worried about Devy and Gwen, too concerned for the Ovaro. It never occurred to him to be concerned for himself. If his time had come, it had come. Fretting wouldn't change things.

He fell asleep without being aware he had done so. A sound snapped him awake and he rose on his elbows. He felt refreshed but his body was a monument to pain. He lifted his buckskin shirt and saw he was black and blue from his waist to his shoulders. Jethro and Toby had worked him over good. He regretted not shooting them in the head instead of the legs.

More sounds filtered through the door. The clang of pots and pans. The clomp of boots on floorboards. Occasional voices. The Hinkles were up and about and having their breakfast.

Fargo did not expect to be fed. He slid off the bed and sat in the chair. When he heard someone outside the room, he stretched his legs out and laced his hands behind his head even though it hurt like hell, and whistled as if he didn't have a care in the world.

Clyde, Arvil and Tyrel had been sent to fetch him. They looked at the bed, then at him, and Clyde grinned. "Mister, you are one tough son of a bitch."

"I'd like a side of bacon and some eggs," Fargo said.

Arvil motioned with his revolver. "Fat chance. The

sun is up and Pa wants you outside. It's time for his special surprise."

Fargo stood up without betraying the torment it caused. "Is this where he pretends I have rabies so he can shoot me like he did your mother?"

All three turned to stone.

"I can't imagine a man doing that to a woman who stuck by him so many years, but then, I'm not your father." Fargo moved toward the door. "All because he wants a younger woman who happened to be someone else's wife."

Clyde and Arvil were glaring. Arvil was maddest, and rasped, "Shut your mouth, you lyin' sack of dung. My pa would never do a thing like that."

"Oh?" Fargo nodded at Tyrel. "Ask your brother there if you don't believe me. He knows it's true."

"Tyrel?" Arvil said, but his brother shook his head.

Clyde grabbed Fargo and propelled him from the room. "Enough of this. We shouldn't keep Pa waitin'."

Fargo had planted a seed. Whether anything would come of it, only time would tell. But it wouldn't hurt to add a little water and fertilizer. "Your mother must not have been much of a wife for your father to get rid of her like that. Or maybe she just wasn't pretty enough for him."

"Shut up, I said!" Arvil fumed, and came at him ready to club him with the Remington.

Clyde seized his arm before it could descend. "Calm down, you lunkhead. He's just tryin' to get your goat. Pa would never do that and you know it."

"Sure," Arvil said, but he did not sound sure.

Tyrel looked more upset than ever.

Grinning, Fargo strolled on out into the sunlight. Another cloudless scorcher of a day was in store. He saw the Ovaro in the corral and it saw him and nickered.

All the Hinkles were on hand. So were Devona and Gwen.

Showing off his tobacco-stained teeth, Leon greeted him warmly. "I trust you're rested up? No hard feelin's about last night? You can't rightly blame my boys after what you did."

"Why would I have hard feelings?" Fargo said. "I'm not the one whose mother you killed."

Leon rocked on his heels like he had been slugged.

Fargo did not let up. "I was just telling your three sons here how you murdered Agnes so you could take Devy into your bed. Arvil doesn't believe me. But I'll bet Agnes never showed any sign of rabies before you killed her. All anyone has is your word she came down with it." Fargo turned to the stunned siblings. "Can any of you prove me wrong? Did your mother ever say she was feeling poorly?"

A roar of fury exploded from Leon Hinkle, and he went berserk. Fargo received a punch to the shoulder and another to the ribs, then doubled over so his back absorbed most of the blows.

Leon swung and swung until he was spent. "How dare you try to turn my boys against me! When they know how much I loved their ma!" He was shaking fiercely, the veins in his temples and neck fit to burst. "But every coon has its moment and you've had yours. Now it's my turn."

Fargo said nothing. He was studying the sons, and he liked what he saw.

Leon bobbed his stubbly chin at the brown hills. "Out there is mile after mile of heat and dust and wild critters with rabies. How long do you reckon you'd last on foot with no water and no gun?"

Fargo shrugged. "There's no telling."

"That's right. You're a frontiersman. You know how to live off the land better than most. You might last a good long while." Leon's smile was vicious. "But how long with my hellhounds on your heels?" He took an old, battered pocket watch from a pocket and opened it. "I'll be sportin' about this and give you a fifteen minute head start."

"That's mighty generous."

Rising, Leon removed Fargo's hat. "You won't be needin' this. All it does is protect your head from the sun. And I need somethin' with your scent on it."

"I can go any direction I want?" Fargo asked.

"So long as it's due south." Leon consulted his watch again. "You now have fourteen minutes and fifty seconds."

9

Skye Fargo crossed the top of the hill and flew down the south slope. He did not think about the burning sun. He did not think about the horrendous heat. He shut out the pain from the beating he had taken. All he thought about were the hellhounds, and the mental ticking of a clock in his head.

Fifteen minutes was no head start at all. Not when the hellhounds could run twice as fast as he could. Not when it would take them only five minutes to cover the ground he covered in his full allotment. Outrunning them was out of the question. Eluding them, with their keen sense of smell, seemed impossible. But of the two options, only the second offered any chance of survival. He must rely on his wits rather than fleetness of foot. He must out think the hairy bastards.

Fargo had an idea. At the bottom of the hill part of the slope had buckled, resulting in a trough some thirty feet long and about six feet wide. He had noticed it the day before when he was spying on the Hinkles and waiting for dark to fall. Noticing landmarks was second nature to him, as it was to any scout.

Three of the fifteen minutes had gone by when Fargo reached the trough. The sides were about four feet high. Quickly, he knelt and clawed at the dirt, digging with a desperation born of self-preservation. Loose earth cascaded down, forming a pile. Dust swirled about his face and clung to his skin and pants. Two more minutes went by. Three minutes. Four.

The cavity was the size Fargo needed it. Standing, he stripped off his buckskin shirt and ran down the trough and out the far end. He went fifteen yards and dropped his shirt, then whirled and raced back into the trough to the hole. Sitting with his back to it, he wriggled backward until his back scraped solid earth and began scooping up the dirt from the pile and re-filling the hole.

He covered his feet. He covered his legs as high as his knees. He had the dirt as high as his chest when the first fierce howls rolled off across the hills. Leon Hinkle had set the hellhounds loose on his trail.

Fargo scooped faster. He had to be extremely care-ful not to dislodge the dirt that already covered him. It was as high as his chin when a savage bray warned him he had almost run out of time. He scooped a few final handfuls, closed his eyes, and smeared the last handful over his face and hair. Then he sat com-pletely still.

None too soon. Footfalls and growls filled the trough. Hellhounds loped past his hiding place, many sniffing noisily, and on out the other end. As they went by, they were so close he could have reached out and touched them. He counted twenty but missed a few, they were so jammed together.

A loud howl pealed, followed by a lot of snapping and snarling and then a loud ripping sound. They had found his shirt and were fighting over it. Whether he lived or died depended on what they did next.

Fargo expected some of the hellhounds to head back up the hill. Others would fan out and try to pick up his scent again. Still others would come back into the trough to sniff around. They were the ones who could spell his doom. If they found him pinned in the hole, he wouldn't last ten seconds.

A shadow flickered across the trough and a big hell-hound padded past. Then another. A third started past but stopped and sniffed at what was left of the pile of dirt. Fargo could see its nostrils flare, see its sides move as it breathed, see the spittle on its fangs when its mouth opened and its tongue lolled out. All it had to do was turn and they would be eye to eye. Nose to the dirt, it started to shift toward the hole.

Howls from down the trough saved him. Hearing them, the hellhound looked over its shoulder, listened a few moments, then ran off down the trough. There was more snarling and snapping, and after that, nothing.

Fargo stayed right where he was. Half an hour went by and he didn't move a muscle. Some of the hellhounds might still be nearby. Even if they weren't, he was too exposed, too vulnerable, out in the open. It was safer right where he was. Cooler, too, since he was spared the worst of the relentless sun.

More time crawled by on snail's feet. Fargo was feeling cramped and stiff and had a kink in his back but he endured the discomfort. His nose itched and he rubbed it against the top of the hole.

Suddenly voices intruded on the quiet. Footsteps came along the edge of the trough above him.

"—don't see why Pa had to send us," Arvil Hinkle was grousing. "Why not Chad or Eli or any of the others? Why is it always us?"

"You and me are the oldest," Clyde Hinkle said. "He trusts us more."

"It's a waste of our time," Arvil said. "That shirt the hellhounds brought back was ripped to hell. Fargo is worm food."

"There wasn't any blood on the shirt," Clyde noted, "so Pa wants us to make sure. Can't say as I blame him. Fargo ain't to be taken lightly."

"Oh, please. He puts on his britches one leg at a time like the rest of us."

"If Pa is so damn concerned," a third Hinkle spoke, "why didn't he come himself instead of triflin' with that Carroway woman?" It was Tyrel.

"They're fixin' to be hitched tomorrow," Clyde said. "There's a lot for him to get ready."

"Like what?" Tyrel angrily replied. "The food? We're doin' all the bakin' and cookin'. Her dress? She'll be wearin' the one she has on. There's nothin' for him to do but sit around makin' cow eyes at her."

Fargo saw their shadows on the opposite side of the trough. They had stopped and were leaning on their rifles.

"Pa has been actin' strange all mornin'," Arvil mentioned. "Ever since that Fargo feller accused him of killin' Ma." He paused. "You don't reckon there's any truth to it, do you?"

Clyde voiced a few choice swear words. "I should blow out your wick for talkin' against Pa. He loved Ma just as much as we did. It must have been awful hard for him to put her out of her misery."

"How about you, brother Tyrel?" Arvil asked.

"I'd rather not say."

One of the shadows started to walk off but stopped when another gestured.

"Hold on there, brother Tyrel," Clyde said. "That look on your face just now. You don't believe that fella's lies, do you?"

"I'm not sayin' they're lies and I'm not sayin' they aren't. All I know is that Ma wasn't sickly when Pa shot her. I talked to her earlier that day and she was fit as a fiddle but upset with Pa over the hellhound business. She always thought it was wrong. And one of the last things she said to me keeps stickin' in my craw."

"What was it?" from Arvil.

"I told her that Pa had mentioned invitin' the widow Carroway over for supper and she looked at me strange. 'Tyrel,' she says, 'when your Pa finally lets you marry, remember one thing. A pretty face can't compare to the woman who takes you for better or worse.'"

"Ma said that?" Clyde said.

"I don't like it. I don't like any of it." Arvil sounded like he was about to cry. "I loved Ma as much as any of you. She was always so kind. So caring. If I thought for a minute Pa really did like Fargo claims—" He didn't finish his statement.

"We'd best keep lookin' for the body." Clyde's shadow moved. "Keep this talk just between us. If word got back to Pa, he'd skin us alive."

Silence claimed the hills, and Fargo relaxed. His back itched but he didn't scratch it. Twice he felt an urge to sneeze and pressed his nose against a knee until the urge faded. His legs cramped terribly but he didn't try to relieve the pain. No matter what, he wasn't moving out of that hole until sunset.

It was one of the longest days of Fargo's life.

Twilight blanketed the land and a few stars had appeared when at long last Fargo uncoiled and pushed the dirt off. He began to stand and fell back down. The circulation in his legs had been cut off and they were tingling like mad. Pain replaced the tingling as he rubbed them and moved them up and down. When he could feel his toes, he gripped the side of the trough and pulled himself erect.

Now that the Hinkles were half-convinced he was dead, he could slip away. It wouldn't take more than a couple of days to reach Carn. He could take a canteen from the general store and fill it at the pump and strike out on foot for the main trail. Yes, he could do all that except for one thing: the Carroways. As long as he had breath in his body, he wouldn't desert them.

Turning, Fargo circled around the hill to the north slope. The trees surrounding the spring were a black blot against the backdrop of deepening darkness. At their center glowed a lantern, and seated near it were two Hinkles, Chad and Eli.

Fargo had seen them at the supper table yesterday. They were two of the scruffier members of the clan whose bathing habits had obviously not been affected by the drought. Chad was puffing on a corncob pipe. Eli was doodling in the dirt with a stick. The planks

Fargo had torn off the shed had not yet been replaced and the sweet smell of water was strong in the dry air.

Licking his dry lips, Fargo glided through the trees to the rear of the shed. Flattening, he crawled around it, moving as slowly as a stalking cougar, and peered past the front corner.

The stick Eli was doodling with wasn't a stick at all. It was the Arkansas Toothpick. Both men wore revolvers and had rifles within easy reach.

"Are you lookin' forward to tomorrow, brother Chad?" Eli asked.

Chad removed his pipe to say, "It's just a day like any other."

"I mean the weddin'. All that food and the cake and fiddle playin' afterward. It should be fun." Eli looked up. "We ain't had a real rip-snortin' hootenanny in a coon's age."

"This won't hardly qualify. There won't be no womenfolk other than the widow, and she belongs to Pa."

"Do you feel the least bit sorry for her? Tyrel does. He told me he thinks Pa is marryin' her too soon after Ma was planted."

"She don't mean diddly to me. I think she should be thankful a man like Pa is stoopin' to take her for his own. As for Tyrel, he always was a mite sissified."

"Ain't that the truth." Eli bent to his doodling.

In two bounds Fargo was up and past the shed. He grabbed the barrel of Chad's rifle and swung. The stock thudded against Chad's head before Chad could do more than blink, and down he went.

Eli's reflexes were faster. Cursing, he was up off the ground in the blink of an eye, slashing the Toothpick low.

Fargo saved his manhood by pivoting on the balls of his feet. Quick as thought, he slammed the rifle against Eli's forehead with a sickening *crack* as Eli pitched onto his face with a loud groan.

Squatting, Fargo listened for outcries from above. When there were none, he slid the Arkansas Toothpick into his ankle sheath, then unbuckled Chad's gun belt and strapped it around his own waist. The revolvers were Smith and Wessons. Fargo preferred a Colt but it wasn't the model that killed a man, it was the slug that came out of the end of the barrel. He checked to ensure they were loaded.

Eli's revolvers were Remingtons and Remington made quality firearms, but they weren't the same caliber as the Smith and Wessons, so he left them. He did take Eli's rifle, a Spencer, and a cartridge belt for it that he slung across his chest.

Fargo could use a shirt but he was foot taller and a lot broader of shoulder than either of them so neither of theirs would fit. He needed a hat, too, but they both wore hats with floppy brims and he would be damned if he would be caught dead in one of those.

From the rim of the hill Fargo saw Hinkles moving about inside the house. Jethro and Toby were playing cards, their crutches at their sides. The Carroways, he figured, must be in the same room as last night. They could keep for a few minutes more. He had something else to do.

For once the hellhounds in the kennel were quiet. Maybe because the packs roaming the hills were also quiet. But that wouldn't last long.

Doubled over, Fargo ran to the corral. The Ovaro's senses were as keen as ever and it came over to the fence and nickered. He glanced at the house but when no one came out to investigate he patted the stallion's neck and moved along the corral to where his saddle blanket, saddle and bridle were draped over the top rail. The Ovaro followed. Climbing inside, he saddled up and led the stallion to the gate.

At that exact instant the front door to the house opened and out stepped Tyrel. He looked mad. He started toward the end of the porch nearest the corral but Arvil came out and said something and they talked in low tones. After a while Tyrel gestured in resignation and they went back in.

Pushing on the gate, Fargo forked leather and rode at a walk in a wide loop that brought him up to the window on the east side of the house. Sliding off, he parted the curtains with the Spencer. A lamp gleamed on a dresser but Devy and Gwen weren't there. He slipped over the sill and over to the door. It was partway open. From down the hall drifted laughter and the tinkle of a glass.

Aware that at any moment someone might discover the Ovaro was missing or go to the spring and find Chad and Eli, Fargo stepped into the hall. To his right another door opened and Leon Hinkle emerged, looking the other way. Instantly Fargo stepped back into the bedroom and darted behind the door. He peered through the crack as several people approached.

Into the room walked Devona, carrying Gwen. Her face was worn and tired and she moved woodenly.

"Get a good night's rest, my dear." Leon Hinkle stopped in the doorway. "Tomorrow you'll see everything in a whole new light."

All Fargo had to do was step past the door and he could blow Leon's brains out, but the patriarch wasn't alone. Clyde and two other sons were behind him and all three were well-armed. In an exchange of lead, a stray bullet might hit the Carroways.

Devy said flatly, "You can't seem to get it through that thick head of yours that I want nothing to do with you. Not after what you did to Brian and Skye."

"You say that now. But in a month or two you'll change your mind." Leon smiled. "You'll grow to care for me as much as my Agnes did."

Fargo heard the bed creak and a drawn-out sigh.

"What does it take to get through to you? I hate you, you bastard. I hate you with every fiber of my being. Dare to lay a hand on me and so help me God, I'll kill you."

"No, you won't," Leon said confidently.

"How can you be so sure?"

Hinkle played his trump card. "Because if you kill

me, my boys will kill you. That would leave your darlin' child all alone in the world. Who will look after her when you're gone?"

"I will, Pa," Clyde said. "I'll look after her real nice. And in three or four years, when she's come of age, I'll take her as my bride."

Devy's groan of despair filled the room. "You're all animals. No better than those vile hellhounds you breed. I pray you get what's coming to you, and I pray I'm around to see it happen."

"Better get some rest," Leon encouraged her. "We want you lookin' your best for the big day tomorrow. I'll have the boys fill the wash tub with hot water so you can take a bath. I like my women to smell fresh and clean."

"Go away," Devy said wearily. "I can't stand any more of you. I honestly can't. If you don't go away, I'll scream."

Chuckling, Leon closed the door.

Devy closed her eyes and slumped forward, one hand on her sleeping daughter. "God in heaven, what did I ever do to deserve this nightmare?"

As silently as a ghost, Fargo crossed the room and clamped a hand over her mouth. "Your nightmare is about to end," he whispered in her ear.

Amazement brought Devona to her feet. Tears flowed, tears of happiness, and she wrapped her arms around him and buried her face in his chest. "You! They told me you were dead!"

"They're going to wish I was," Fargo whispered. "Right now we have to burn the breeze. You go first."

Devy climbed out the window. Fargo handed Gwen out, then gave Devy a boost onto the Ovaro. She took Gwen and held her on her lap. Fargo swung up and reined the stallion around.

The night was still quiet. He walked the pinto for half a mile, then brought it to a trot but only for a short distance. The motion woke Gwen up but when her mother assured her all was well, she went right back to sleep. They had traveled a couple of miles when Devona placed a hand on his arm.

"I didn't think to ask. Where are we heading? To my farm? Or the trail to Fort Bridger?"

"Carn."

Devy's fingernails bit into his skin. "The last time we were there we were lucky to make it out alive. I trust you have a good reason?"

"I have a plan." That was all Fargo told her. She would think he was foolish if she knew the truth. He couldn't leave. Not now. Not after all the Hinkles had done to him. Not after being beaten and having the hellhounds sicced on him. The Hinkles had a lot to answer for, Leon Hinkle most of all, and he was going to see to it they paid in full. He couldn't risk letting them gain control of the area. Power and influence coupled with their unscrupulous ways would spawn a truly hideous breed. Fargo wasn't about to allow them to cause more harm. And if that meant killing every last one of the sons of bitches, so be it.

The ride was uneventful. Well before dawn Fargo wound out of the hills onto the grassy plain. Ahead reared the inky silhouette of the town, the buildings looming like gigantic tombstones. He skirted Carn and reined up at the back door to the house with the stone fence. Devy and Gwen were dozing. He was reluctant to wake them but he had to.

Instructing Devy to keep Gwen there, Fargo went in. The reek was only slightly worse than it had been on his earlier visit. He made a sweep of all the ground floor rooms before going up to the second floor. Taking a deep breath, he opened the door to the dead man's bedroom. He was glad it was too dark to see how decomposed the body had become. After covering it with the quilt and the sheets, he opened a side window, carried the body over, and dropped it out. Leaving the window open, he went out, closing the door behind him.

From a bed in another room Fargo stripped another quilt, rolled it up, and wadded it against the bottom of the door to the dead man's bedroom to help reduce the smell. He took several pillows downstairs with him.

Devona and Gwen were nervously waiting for him to return. He gave Devona the pillows, then saw that they made themselves comfortable in a sitting room.

"Aren't you going to lie down with us, Mr. Fargo?" Gwen asked when he headed back out.

"My horse comes before I do," Fargo explained. He attempted to lead the Ovaro inside but it balked. Again and again he brought it to the doorway and again and again it shied away. But he couldn't leave it outside, not with hellhounds running loose and rabid animals everywhere.

He looked at the door, at the two steps leading up to it, trying to figure out why the stallion was so skittish. Was it because the steps were so small? Or became the doorway was so narrow? He remembered seeing a towel on a hook in the kitchen, and brought it out. The Ovaro snorted but didn't act up when he covered its eyes. Gripping the bridle, he guided it indoors without any difficulty, pressing down on its neck so its head cleared the lintel.

The Carroways had saved a pillow for him. Fargo placed it on the floor near a window and tried to sleep but he wasn't tired. He had dozed most of the day away in the hole in the trough. He occupied himself reviewing the layout of the town. Which buildings were where, and how high they were. It would soon be important.

A floorboard squeaked and Devona's hand brushed his neck. She was hunkered beside him, her hair spilling over her face. "I can't sleep."

"Makes two of us," Fargo said.

"Gwen is out to the world. I thought you might like to find somewhere quiet so we can talk?"

In a small room under the stairs were shelves lined with books. Against the far wall stood a sofa, and Fargo had no sooner taken a seat than Devona straddled his legs as she had done at her house. "I thought you wanted to talk?" he said.

"Is it safe, do you think?"

"It should be." Fargo doubted the Hinkles would get there much before noon. The house was empty save for them, and with the doors and windows closed and locked, rabid animals couldn't get at them. Rabid people were another matter but he would hear if someone tried to break in.

Devy was running her fingers through his hair. "I want to forget for a while. I want to forget the terrible things I've been through. I want to forget Hinkle and his wretched brood." Her kiss wasn't soft or tender or romantic. It was hard and hungry and ripe with need.

The tension drained from Fargo's sinews like water from a sieve. His desire kindled, he felt himself harden, felt a familiar ache in his groin. He cupped her left breast and Devy groaned. He cupped the other and she squirmed in his lap and nibbled on his ear.

"Do you know what I like about making love to you?"

Fargo could not begin to guess.

"You're not like most men. My Brian was the sweetest husband who ever lived but in bed he was always too quick and too rough. He couldn't wait to get it over with. You, on the other hand, like to take your sweet time. It makes all the difference."

"You talk too much."

Their mouths melted into one. Devy's breasts were against his chest and her fingers delicately rubbed his temples. Fargo placed his hands on her thighs and kneaded them.

The room around them seemed to recede. It was just the two of them, with their pounding hearts and their rising passion.

Twisting, Fargo lowered Devy onto her back. Her legs parted and she wrapped them around his waist. Her hands rose to hook behind his neck. "You're the most amazing man I've ever met."

Fargo pulled her close. They were dusty and sweaty but they didn't care. He licked her throat and she arched her back. Her tongue found his ear and swirled the lobe, her heavy breaths causing his skin to prickle and his pole to become as rigid as the mast of a ship. He felt her hand close around it and a lump formed in his throat.

"Don't keep me waiting," Devy cooed. "I want you inside me."

For once Fargo had no interest in prolonging his lovemaking as long as possible. Not with imminent death hanging over their heads. He unbuckled his belt and jiggled his manhood free and she gently enfolded the tip and stroked him from stem to stern.

"Now," Devy huskily begged. "Please! Now!"

Slowly inserting himself, Fargo paused to savor the delight her wet, rippling sheath provoked. Her long, velvety legs clamped tighter, her ankles scraped the small of his back. At his initial stroke, she rose up to meet him, grinding her hips to heighten their mutual pleasure.

"Here we go," Fargo said with a grin. Gripping her hips, he plumbed her womanhood. As the seconds went by, he stroked harder and faster, always harder and faster, until their bodies were slapping together like clapping hands and the sofa bounced to an earthquake only they experienced.

"I'm almost there!" Devy mewed.

Fargo found a nipple and pinched it. She quivered, her eyes rolling in their sockets. The signs were unmistakable. He did not think he could gush quite so soon but then she did something with her inner walls, she gripped him somehow, and exploded like a cannon.

"Yes!" Devona whispered. "Yes! Yes! Yes!"

Fargo could not agree more.

10

The morning dawned cooler than any in recent weeks. Skye Fargo stood on the front porch and breathed deep of the welcome crisp air. He had almost forgotten what it felt like.

The sun was a golden sliver on the horizon but the sky had brightened enough for Fargo to see Carn's lifeless street and the buildings, all as dead as sepulchers. He walked down the footpath to the gate. The dead dog was still there and the maggots were having a feast. He gazed south, remembering the sign at the fork that started his odyssey into hell. Sometimes the forks not taken were the best.

Something moved at the base of the stone fence. Fargo looked, and saw a rabbit. It saw him at the same time. Instead of bounding off in fear as rabbits normally did, this one uttered a thin shriek that Fargo would never have thought rabbits capable of, and came toward him. The white flecks around its mouth weren't visible until it was almost to the gate.

A rabbit. A lowly, timid rabbit. Fargo shot it with the Spencer and it tumbled to a stop with its long ears quivering and its legs jerking spasmodically.

Devona ran out on the porch, wide-eyed and panicked, her hair in a tangle, the top of her dress partially undone. "What is it?" she cried in confusion. "Why did you shoot?"

"A rabid animal." Fargo did not tell her what it had been. "Go back inside. See if there's any food in the kitchen. I want you and Gwen gone within the hour." He would give them that much but not a minute more, not when hellhounds might appear at any time.

Fargo climbed onto the stone fence. Everywhere he looked, in all that vast domain of withered grass and brown hills, there wasn't a single trace of life. Between the drought and the rabies and the hellhounds, a lush paradise had been transformed into a barren wasteland. He waited to be sure the shot hadn't drawn unwanted attention, and when Carn remained as dead as a cemetery, he hopped down and went in.

The scent of brewing coffee wafted down the hall. Fargo heard sizzling and the clang of a pan and his stomach growled at the prospect of eating for the first time in thirty-six hours.

Gwen was at the kitchen table. Smiling sleepily, she greeted him with a cheerful, "Good morning. Ma says we're leaving soon."

"The two of you are," Fargo clarified. He set the Spencer on the table and sank into a chair across from her.

"Aren't you coming with us? Ma will be awful disappointed. She's taken a shine to you."

Devona nearly dropped a skillet.

"I need to stay," Fargo said. "I'm expecting company."

"It's those mean men, isn't it? You're going to stay and kill them if you can. Them, and their mean dogs."

"Someone has to."

"Why not let the army do it? That's what they're paid to do, Ma says. To kill bad people like those Hinkles."

"Some things a man has to do himself."

"Just don't get hurt. I like you, too. You're the nicest man I've ever met besides my pa. If you wanted to live with us, my ma says she wouldn't mind. Me either."

About to crack an egg, Devona glanced at her pride

and joy. "That's enough, Gwendolyn. Don't pester Mr. Fargo. He has a lot on his mind right now."

"Killing bad men," Gwen said.

The pantry was amply stocked. In addition to the coffee and eggs, Devy had found enough flour, salt, canned goods and jerked beef to feed a regiment. She had also discovered a jug of water.

Fargo downed a couple of cups of coffee before the food arrived. He was so famished he ate six eggs, two flapjacks, a slab of beef, two slices of bread, and for dessert, a rare treat: canned pears.

Giggling, Gwen watched him spear a pear with his fork. "Goodness gracious, you should be fit to burst. You eat more than my pa and all my uncles put together."

What would she think, Fargo wondered, if he told her he was still hungry? Too much food would make him sluggish, though, and he needed to be as sharp as a straight razor for later. Everyone had finished eating and he was sipping one last cup of coffee when he looked at them and announced, "Time for you to go. Take my horse and ride to the main trail, then head east until you reach the fort."

Devona looked down at the table. "We're not leaving."

"I thought we had this worked out," Fargo told her. "It's for your own good. I can't promise I can keep Gwen and you safe once the Hinkles and their pets show up. Go while you still can."

"No."

Fargo was becoming annoyed. She had never let on she would pull this kind of stunt. "What about Gwen? Do it for her if for no other reason. You've already lost your husband and your son. You don't want to lose your daughter, too."

"We can help you. Find me a rifle. I know how to shoot and I'm not afraid to squeeze the trigger."

Fargo had sensed she was becoming too attached to him, and here was the proof. "I can't watch my back and yours at the same time. You'll be doing me a favor by riding out. Please, Devona."

Devy met his gaze. "No. And that's final. If you won't let me help, then we'll hide somewhere until it's over." She nodded at the stairs. "I saw a door to an attic in the upstairs hall. That should do."

"This isn't necessary," Fargo insisted. He had half a mind to tie them to the Ovaro and give the stallion a smack on the rump.

"To me it is. You've stood by us when we needed help. You've put your life at risk on our behalf. We owe you more than we can ever repay."

"You don't owe me a thing. I was only doing what any man would."

"Any man?" Devy shook her head. "Not one in a hundred would do what you've done. Most would have been too busy saving their own hides. You're an exceptional man whether you admit it or not."

"Damn it." Fargo fought his rising anger. "If I go down, there's no one to protect you. The Hinkles will tear the town apart looking for you and they'll find you. Leon will take you for his woman and a few years from now Gwen will be forced to marry one of his sons. Is that what you want?"

"Of course not. But what kind of person would I be if I ran out? How could I ever hold my head high? Men don't have a monopoly on self-respect. I owe it to myself to stay." Devy tenderly put a hand on her daughter's shoulder. "As for Gwen, she's old enough to understand. I can't be an example to her if I don't live the way I'm always telling her we should."

Gwen smiled and nodded. "Whatever Ma wants is fine by me."

Fargo could see that arguing was pointless. And he had a lot to do before the Hinkles arrived. "Check the attic and make sure it's free of bats. They get rabies like everything else." He stood. "And I want your word if I'm killed, you'll take my horse and ride like hell."

"You have it," Devona pledged.

A gun cabinet was in one corner of the parlor. It held a Colt Model 1855 repeating rifle and an English-made shotgun. In a drawer underneath were boxes of ammunition. With the Colt rifle and a shotgun under one arm and the Spencer in his other hand, Fargo walked into Carn to prepare.

Since he had checked the general store for firearms the other day, he went directly to the corral behind the stable. The man who had tried to steal the Ovaro was still prone in the dust, half his face chewed away. Beside him was the Spencer. Now Fargo had two. He entered the church. No one had cut down the parson and the body was riper than ever. Practically choking on the stench, he slashed the rope and dragged the rotting corpse out back.

The steeple was the highest point in town. From it, Fargo had an unobstructed view of the hills. He left the horse thief's Spencer in the belfry and climbed down. Next highest was the roof of the feed and grain store. There, Fargo placed the Colt repeating rifle and a box of ammunition in a corner overlooking the street. Shotguns were only effective at short range so Fargo hid it in the shadows in the barber shop. From there he went to the saloon. He searched under the bar and smiled when he set eyes on a sawed-off double-barreled shotgun and a box of shells. He loaded the scattergun and laid it to one side of the bat-wing doors.

As yet, Fargo hadn't seen a living soul. Or a rabid one. He walked back behind the bar, selected an unopened bottle of whiskey, and took it out to a chair on the boardwalk. Eli's Spencer across his lap, he opened the bottle and tilted it to his mouth. It was early yet but he was entitled. Before the day was over he would be fighting for his life, and there was a very real chance he wouldn't live to see the dawn.

Sitting there, Fargo suddenly realized that for the first time in days he wasn't sweating. The sun was well above the horizon but the temperature hadn't climbed more than a degree or two. It must be a sign that the weather was about to change.

Suddenly he heard a thump. It came from the narrow space between the saloon and the next building and was repeated several times, each time louder than the last. He set down the bottle and raised the Spencer. To him it sounded like someone was hitting the wall.

Into the sunlight staggered a sickly pale apparition in the throes of full-blown rabies. As thin as a broom, the man could barely stand. The skin on his face had shrunk in on itself, lending him the visage of a walking skeleton. Convulsions shook his ravaged body. Some were mild. Some were severe. From his throat came a cross between a grunt and a growl. "Unnnhhh. Unnnhhh."

Fixing the Spencer's sights on the man's head, Fargo said, "Looking for something?"

Twitching and jerking, the man slowly turned. His thin lips curled back. It made him seem like he was grinning. "Unnnhhh. Unnnhhh," he croaked, and lurched toward the chair, a walking skull wearing a lunatic grin.

Fargo shot him. He did not give the body a second glance. "A toast," he said out loud, reaching for the bottle, "to all those who think life makes sense." The whiskey seared his throat and landed with a pleasantly warm explosion in his stomach.

In his time Fargo had seen a lot of bloodshed, a lot of death and butchery. He had stood over what was left of white men mutilated and scalped by hostiles, over red men carved into pieces by whites for no reason other than the color of their skin. In Arizona he helped bury a muleskinner Apaches had tied to a wagon wheel and lit a fire under. In Texas he saw a farmer the Comanches had done unspeakable things to. He had seen whites do horrible things to whites, red men do horrible things to red men. It could not help but affect him.

Fargo sometimes wondered why he was always risking his hide for people he hardly knew. Whenever that happened, whenever he started to question himself, he would think of that muleskinner or the farmer or all the other atrocities and random acts of bloodshed, and his doubts always evaporated. As Devona had said, what kind of person would he be if he did not do what he could to keep things like that from happening?

Shaking himself, Fargo stood. Now was not the time to become mired in thought. Leaving the bottle on the chair, he hurried south to the house with the stone fence.

Devy and Gwen were on the porch. "We were getting worried," Devy said. "We heard a shot."

"It's time you were up in the attic. Take as much food as you want and what's left of the water."

"It's already up there." Devy grinned. "But we don't want to go up yet. If we had a gun, we could help. Maybe shoot a few hellhounds and Hinkles for you."

"We?"

"I'm not leaving my ma's side and we're not leaving yours," Gwen declared. "We've talked it over."

"I see. Have you talked over what it's like to be dead? Because if the hellhounds spot you, they'll break down the door to get in. Just like they broke through your front door at the farm."

Devy shook her head. "You're trying to scare us but it won't work. We've made up our minds. After all you've done for us, we're doing all we can for you."

Fargo could see why Brian Carroway married her. She was attractive. She enjoyed making love. And most important of all, she stuck by those she cared for through thick and thin. "Leave the Hinkles and the hellhounds to me." He drew one of the Smith and Wessons and handed it to Devona. "Use this only if they get into the house." He turned to leave.

Suddenly Gwen shot to her feet. "Did you feel that just now? Where did it come from?"

Fargo had indeed felt it. A gust of cool wind on his face. It was there and then it was gone. He looked up. Several small clouds were scuttling across the sky out of the northwest.

"Wouldn't it be wonderful if it rained?" Devona said excitedly. "We haven't had any in so long, I've forgotten what it's like."

Fargo had mixed feelings. Rain would break the back of the drought, but it would also cloak the approach of the Hinkles and the hybrids, and that was the last thing he needed. "I'll be in the church."

"Be careful," Devy urged. "I would hate for anything to happen to you."

"Get to the attic," Fargo said, knowing full well she wouldn't. When it was over, if they survived, he would sit her down and explain that while he was flattered by her feelings for him, he could never replace Brian in her affections. He was too much of a wanderer to ever stay in one place, or with one woman, for very long.

More clouds drifted overhead, the most Fargo had seen since he left Seattle. For every two or three white fluffy ones there was a slate gray cloud that hinted Devona's wish might come true. The breeze was steady now, and growing stronger, another harbinger of the tantrum nature would throw.

The sound of pounding reached Fargo's ears. He thought another madman might be to blame, but the more he listened, the more convinced he became it was a loose shutter on one of the houses. He passed the feed and grain, the barber shop, the saloon. He had left the doors of the church open to air it out and much of the reek was gone.

The belfry was cramped. The only place to sit was on an inner ledge. He leaned Eli's Spencer against the bell and armed himself with the horse thief's rifle. Each held seven cartridges in a tubular magazine that fit into the butt. Spencers were accurate out to moderate distance but he still liked Henrys better. They held more rounds, for one thing, sixteen if you had one in the chamber. And Henrys did not need to be manually cocked, like Spencers.

Fargo concentrated on the hills to the north. That was the direction the Hinkles would come from. But it might be a while yet. He made himself comfortable, one leg bent, an elbow on his knee. He saw Devy and Gwen still on the porch. They were watching him, and waved.

Fargo did not wave back. They had to get it through their heads they were making a mistake. They had handicapped him by staying, and their stubbornness might prove costly.

Another gust of wind stirred his hair. He gazed to the west, and blinked. A bank of gray clouds lined the horizon. Spawned over the far off Pacific Ocean, they spelled relief for the water-parched region.

A howl keened on the wind. Fargo straightened and turned to the hills and there they were, twenty to twenty-five hellhounds in loose formation. Their big leader let loose with another howl and was mimicked by half a dozen others. They were smack on the Ovaro's trail. Soon they would reach the spot where Fargo had reined wide to bypass Carn. He had to turn them before they reached it or Devona and Gwen would find themselves up to their necks in fangs and claws.

Fargo elevated the Spencer's rear sight. He was not as expert with a Spencer as he was with a Henry so he wasn't surprised when his first shot kicked up dirt fifteen feet in front of the hybrids. He compensated, aimed, and fired again. Just as he squeezed the trigger, the big hellhound at the front of the pack swerved. The slug meant for the leader struck a hellhound behind it and the animal tumbled into the brown grass and did not get up.

Again Fargo aimed. Again he fired. A second hellhound sprawled into oblivion. The rest scattered, loping toward town in pairs and threes. Fargo emptied the first Spencer and dropped two more of the beasts. Grabbing the other Spencer, he banged off several more shots before the hellhounds reached the buildings.

Turning, Fargo swiftly descended the ladder. He had a few rungs left to go when a growl filled the church and a hellhound came racing around a pew, its claws clacking on the wood floor. Hanging by one hand, Fargo leveled the Spencer and fired. The hellhound yipped as the slug cored its hairy chest.

Fargo dropped the rest of the way. He ran to the back door and slammed it shut in the bristling muzzles of four snarling hybrids. He fired through it and heard a squeal of pain.

He was halfway to the front when three more of the hairy brutes came charging in. He fired the last two rounds in the Spencer and brought one of the hellhounds down. The others never slowed, never showed the slightest fear. He was not conscious of letting go of the Spencer but suddenly the Smith and Wesson was in his hand, spewing smoke and lead. He banged off four, five, six shots, and in the ear-ringing silence that followed, he holstered the smoking revolver, snatched up the Spencer, and ran to the front doors.

The street was deserted but hellhounds were out there, Fargo knew, lurking in the shadows. He reloaded the Spencer, then the Smith and Wessons. It was the work of seconds, his fingers flew so fast.

The saloon was catty-corner from the church. To reach it, he must cross sixty feet of open space. He was out and down the steps in a rush. A hybrid appeared near the feed and grain but he did not have a clear enough shot. Another snarled at him from the corner of the general store. Then a pair of hellhounds vaulted a picket fence and came for him with their maws agape. He sent a slug into each but only one went down. The other was coming flat-out, its head down, its fangs bared. He fired, fed another round into the Spencer, fired again and blew out its brains when it was only six feet from him.

Howls rose from all sides.

Fargo ran. He made it to the saloon, exchanged the Spencer for the scattergun, and spun. Hellhounds were almost to the boardwalk. He let them have it with both barrels. The twin booms were as loud as cannon blasts, the aftermath as devastating. Bodies and parts of bodies lay in a wide swath.

Reloading, Fargo stuffed the box of ammo in his pocket. The hybrids had stopped howling and growling. His back to the wall, he sidled to the south corner in time to see the hindquarters of a hellhound vanish at the rear.

Behind him, claws scuffed the boardwalk. Fargo whipped around and squeezed both triggers. A hellhound had launched itself at his back and the blast caught it full in the face. Buckshot at that range could take a man's head off and it did just that to the beast. All that was left was a stump where the neck had been.

Fargo reloaded. He had lost count of how many he killed. There had to be a lot left, though, and more could arrive at any minute. Then there were the Hinkles. He must dispose of the hellhounds so he could deal with their masters. Somehow he must draw the hybrids into the open.

It was then that the wind shrieked the length of the street, raising small dust devils. Fargo had been so intent on staying alive, he hadn't noticed that gray clouds now covered half the sky and would soon cover the rest. The temperature had dropped ten degrees or more, and the scent of moisture was strong. Any other time, he would have been glad.

Running into the saloon, Fargo left the scattergun on a chair and snatched up the Spencer. He had an idea but whether it would work was a long shot. He needed a ladder, and several were for sale out front of the general store. He made it across the street unmolested, chose one high enough, and carried it into the gap between the saloon and the barber shop.

Leaning the ladder against the saloon, Fargo climbed to the roof and moved to the false front. No hellhounds were in sight but they had to have seen him go between the buildings. As far as they knew, he was still there, and when he did not come back out, they might venture from hiding to find him.

Waiting was hard. Fargo had more patience than most men, but every second that ticked by brought the Hinkle clan a second closer to Carn. He refrained from peeking over the false front to see what the hybrids were up to; it would ruin everything if one spotted him.

He watched the clouds devour the sky as if starved, dark tendrils writhing and coiling like thick snakes. The smell of rain grew by the minute. He could almost taste it. Off to the west a misty veil covered a half-mile front. It was rain, and soon a lot more would fall.

From below came a loud sniff. It was repeated several times, and then came a loud growl.

Fargo crawled to the lip. Three hellhounds were sniffing around at the bottom of the ladder. Others were slinking into the gap from both ends. It was working but he must not be hasty. He must bide his time until hybrids crammed the gap from end to end.

The moment came. Rising on his elbows, Fargo smiled in grim satisfaction. He sighted on a hellhound near the street and cored its brain, then shot another next to it. Shifting, he killed two at the rear. His purpose was to block off the ends so the rest couldn't escape but they had steel springs for legs and several easily vaulted over the bodies before he could kill more. He poured lead down, emptying the Spencer and the Smith and Wesson, and when the gunsmoke cleared, there were six fewer hellhounds left to terrorize the countryside.

Fargo reloaded and climbed down the ladder. The street was deserted again. He looked south toward the house but did not see Devona and Gwen.

Movement near the stable drew him in that direction. He got as far as the corral without spotting a hellhound. The sky was completely overcast by now, and the rain front to the west had broadened to a mile. Flashes of lightning pierced it, accompanied by the distant rumble of thunder.

Fargo glanced to the north. Even though he had been expecting it, the sight he beheld made his pulse quicken. More hellhounds had arrived and were clustered on top of the hill nearest town.

With them were the Hinkles.

11

The air crackled with the buildup of the impending storm. Premature twilight cast the blighted land in shadow as the clouds grew darker and darker. Skye Fargo had been in the church belfry for close to half an hour waiting for the attack that was yet to come. The Hinkles had not moved from the hilltop.

Shortly after Fargo spotted them, he saw Leon Hinkle move partway down the slope and raise a hand to his mouth. A long, shrill note trilled, a note produced by a whistle of some kind, and out of Carn loped the hellhounds Fargo had not yet killed, to join those the Hinkles brought with them.

Over two dozen were awaiting the final signal. There were just as many hybrids now as there had been initially, plus the Hinkles to deal with. Fargo was no better off than he had been. He considered taking Devona and Gwen and riding hell bent for leather but he did not consider it long. The hellhounds would overtake them before they went a mile, and in the open, against so many, he stood no chance at all. He must make his fight in Carn. He must make the Hinkles come to him, and once they did, he must do as he had done earlier and always stay on the move to deny them the chance to trap and surround him. For once they did, he would be overwhelmed, leaving Devy and Gwen at their less than tender mercies.

Fargo had a hunch he did not have much longer to wait. The Hinkles could not afford to hold off until nightfall and lose the advantage their numbers gave them. If they were going to attack, they must do it before too many more minutes passed.

As if Leon Hinkle had the exact same thought at the exact same moment, he stepped to the same spot where he had stood when he called the hellhounds, and whistled again. This time, he pointed at the town, then cried out loud enough for Fargo to hear, "Kill! Kill! Kill!"

Howling with bloodlust, the hybrids swarmed down the slope.

Fargo tucked a Spencer to his right shoulder. He had the range, and none of his shots missed. Seven times he fired. Seven hellhounds fell. Swapping the empty Spencer for the other, he killed two more before they reached Carn.

He had closed all the doors before climbing to the belfry. By the time he reached the bottom of the ladder, he could hear fierce snarls and the grinding of fangs at the front and back of the building. The doors were stout and it was unlikely the hybrids could break them down. They would wait out there for him to make a break for it. Or until the Hinkles arrived and broke the doors down.

Fargo ran to a window on the east side. Near it on the floor were the shotgun and the scattergun. He had brought them with him in anticipation of this very moment. Now, setting the Spencer down, he quietly opened the window and stuck his head out. All the hellhounds were at the front and back.

He had rigged a sling for the shotgun using rope, and now he slung it over his left shoulder and laid his hands on the scattergun. The hybrids were making enough racket to mask the sound of his sliding over the sill and dropping lightly to the ground. Cautiously, he moved forward.

Five hellhounds were snapping and clawing at the front doors. They did not see him step around the corner. They did not notice when he tucked the scattergun's rounded stock to his hip. He took a few more steps to be sure and cut loose with first one barrel, then the next. The buckshot ripped through them like grapeshot. Only two were left standing. True to their savage natures, they howled and bounded toward him, straight into the twin-barrels of the shotgun.

Reloading both weapons on the run, Fargo sprinted for the saloon. A glance at the rear of the church showed more hybrids streaming around it. He also saw a two-legged silhouette and the dull glint of metal. He weaved just as a rifle cracked and a leaden hornet buzzed past his right ear.

He darted into the saloon but did not stop. Hurrying out the back door, he turned right, into the gap between the saloon and the barbershop. To reach the ladder he had to jump over the bodies of the hybrids he had slain earlier.

From the roof Fargo spied several Hinkles working their way down the other side of the street. Several more were on his side, peering into every window and doorway.

Clyde Hinkle came from near the church, Arvil and Chad flanking him. Clyde had a normal hound on a leash. The dog had found the scent and was straining toward the saloon.

Fargo needed them closer. He ran to the rear of the building, leaned out over the lip, and trained the shotgun on the back door. He did not have long to wait before the hound emerged, sniffing furiously, with Clyde right behind.

"Where is he, boy? Where is that miserable son of a bitch."

Hoping to catch Arvil and Chad in the same blast, Fargo held his fire. But as luck would have it, Clyde glanced up and their eyes met over the shotgun's long barrels.

"Chad! Arvil! He's on—!"

Fargo let Clyde have a barrel in the face, then gave the hound the same treatment. No one appeared in the doorway. Up and down the street shouts and howls broke out. Hinkles and hellhounds would converge from all over. He must not be there when they did.

The roofs of the barbershop and the saloon were the same height. It was simple for him to jump from one to the other. He was at the apex of his leap when a brilliant bolt of lighting lit the heavens, and as if that were nature's cue, the sky opened up and down came a torrent of large, pelting drops. Within seconds visibility was reduced to twice the length of his arm.

Fargo nearly lost his balance on the suddenly slick saloon roof. He ran to the south wall, slung the shotgun and the scattergun over his arms, and lowered himself over the side. As thunder crashed he dangled a few seconds, then dropped.

The rain drenched him to the skin but he didn't mind. He relished the cool, wet feel, and wished he could stand there and savor the sensation. But with so many enemies out for his hide, he had to keep moving. Carrying the shotguns, he did the last thing the Hinkles would expect. He dashed to the middle of the street, and squatted.

The downpour was a blessing in more ways than one. It smothered his scent so the hellhounds couldn't sniff him out. It masked him from the Hinkles so unless they were a few feet away, they wouldn't recognize him. He could walk down the street with little fear of being spotted. Which was exactly what he did with the scattergun in hand.

Fargo had a mental map of the town in his head. He knew about where the general store should be and made for it. Suddenly another bolt of lighting lit up the entire town. It also revealed a Hinkle, crouched to his right. He could not tell which one it was. Not that it mattered. He loosed both barrels. The next flash revealed the man flat on his back with half his chest blown away.

To the east a rifle spanged and a slug buzzed like an angry hornet. Zigzagging, Fargo sprinted to the general store, shoved on the door, and threw himself onto his belly. From deeper inside a revolver cracked twice and wood slivers stung his cheek. Drawing the Smith and Wesson, he fired at the gun flash. At his third shot someone cried out and a dry goods display crashed to the floor with a man sprawled across it.

It was Jethro, without his crutch. They had applied a splint to his leg so he could walk. Where Jethro's right eye had been was a bullet hole. Fargo started to turn, then stiffened. From under Jethro's body poked a familiar revolver; his own Colt.

Unbuckling the Smith and Wesson, Fargo hid it under a pile of blankets. The shotgun, too. He no longer had need of them. The Colt and the scattergun would suffice. He unstrapped his gun belt from around Jethro's waist and strapped it around his own.

Another flash of lightning lit the front window, impaling a Hinkle in its glare. The man was looking across the street, not inside, and did not see Fargo dart behind the counter.

Boots clomped, and someone coughed. "Jethro? I can't spot Pa or any of the others anywhere. What do we do?"

Fargo rose high enough to see Toby Hinkle limping down the aisle.

"Brother Jethro? I saw you duck in here before the storm hit. Where in hell are you?"

"He's dead." Fargo rose higher.

"You!" Astonishment rooted the young Hinkle in place. "Pa promised Gwen to whoever brings him your head, and I aim to be the one to get her!" Hobbling to the left, he swung the barrel of his rifle up.

Fargo squeezed the scattergun's right trigger, then reloaded, waiting for another lightning bolt to light up the interior so he could warily roll the body over.

Toby was still alive, his mouth a dark smear of gushing blood. "Damn you," he gurgled, spitting droplets. "I hope my kin gut you and strangle you with your own innards."

"Who has my Henry?"

"Go to hell. You think I'll tell you? You stinkin',

rotten son of a—" A fit of coughing ended Toby's epithets and his life.

Fargo groped in the gloom for the fallen rifle. It turned out to be a Jennings Magazine Rifle, as they were called. It had a tubular magazine and an unusual ring trigger. To fire it, a shooter had to push the ring forward so a round was fed from the magazine, then cock the rifle and pull the trigger to the rear so the cartridge was inserted into the chamber. Then the ring had to be pulled again for the rifle to go off. It was much too complicated a system and explained why the Jennings was not popular on the frontier. He held onto it anyway.

Another bolt from the sky lit up the street and the boards, and Fargo saw hellhounds at the window, staring in at him. A lot of hellhounds, more than he could count in the brief flare of light. It faded, and he rose and backed toward the counter. They stared, unmoving, for all of ten seconds. Then one howled and they were at the doorway, jostling one another in their savage eagerness to tear at his throat.

Fargo leveled the scattergun and gave them both barrels. It momentarily checked their charge. The rest came streaming in as he vaulted up onto the counter. He got off two shots from the Jennings, reversed his grip, and clubbed hybrids as fast as they sprang at him. Two, three, four went tumbling to the floor, and the rest backed off and crouched, growling fiercely.

Hurling the Jennings at them, Fargo spun and leaped down. He reloaded the scattergun as he ran and heard the scrabbling of their claws close on his heels. Suddenly whirling, he fired. It broke their rush but they would be on him again within moments. He ran on, fumbling at his pocket for more shells.

A narrow hall led to small rooms at the back. He ducked into the first open doorway and slammed the door after him. He was in a storeroom. Crates and containers were stacked high but there was space enough to sink to his knees facing the door and upend the ammo box next to him so he could grab fresh shells quickly.

The hellhounds slammed into the door hard enough to jar it on its hinges. Over and over they battered at the barrier that stood between them and their intended prey, their snarls and howls eclipsing the storm's din.

It was possible the door would hold but Fargo couldn't stay there forever; more Hinkles might show up. He aimed at a spot about four feet above the floor and emptied the scattergun into the door, one barrel after the other. Yips and yowls of agony greeted the blasts.

The hellhounds thrust themselves into the gaping holes made by the buckshot, clawing and biting at the wood in a mad attempt to reach him. Fargo reloaded and fired. More fell but there were plenty left, and now their rage knew no bounds. They were almost inside. Two of their number had their bodies half in and half out and were clawing at the floor for the leverage they needed to squeeze their hindquarters through.

Fargo reloaded, fired, reloaded, fired, again and again and again, until his ears were hammering and the burnt odor of gunpowder filled his nose and throat and the storeroom was filled with so much gunsmoke, he couldn't see the door. He reached down for more shells but his hand camp up empty. There were none left. In the sudden lull the only sound was the patter of rain on the roof.

Fargo dropped the scattergun and drew his Colt. Rising, he swatted at the gunsmoke. Between the buckshot and the hybrids little was left of the door. Dead and dying hellhounds, or parts of them, choked the doorway and the hall. A pool of blood inches-deep was rapidly spreading.

He hastened down the hallway to the back door, made sure no surprises were waiting, and went out. The driving rain felt better than ever. Leaning against the wall, he let it wash over him. He was sick of the killing. He did it because he had to, because he had no choice, not because he liked it.

On the frontier survival came at a price. It was not like back East where people could go their whole life long and never have a gun pointed at them or have a hostile try to lift their scalps or a wild beast try to eat them. Out here a man could not turn the other cheek or he would have it ripped from his face. It was kill or be killed, and Fargo liked being alive.

All the death and dying he had seen, he never dwelled on it. He did what he had to in order to survive, and once it was over with, he put it from his mind and went on with his life.

Crashing thunder roused Fargo out of himself. He shook his head, annoyed at his carelessness. He wasn't sure how many Hinkles and hellhounds were left but he had to stay alert. His life wasn't the only one at stake. There were the Carroways to think of.

Fargo headed south, slipping from building to building until he came to the feed and grain. It had a loading platform at the back for farm wagons to pull up to, and a door that hung open. Crouching, he darted inside and paused with his back to the wall. All was quiet, but in the glare of another display of lightning he saw wet footprints. Someone else was there.

He glided forward, stopping every few yards to cock his head and strain his ears. Shadows mantled the farm implements and tool displays. Hunkered behind a plow, he scanned the main room.

The stairs were at the front, to the right of the door he had busted down the morning he arrived.

About a dozen feet away was a harrow. Fargo had taken two steps toward it when flame and smoke stabbed the dark and a slug missed him by a hair. He dived and rolled and came up shooting, two swift blasts at the corner the shot came from. There was no outcry, no sound of a falling body.

Fargo raised his head a little higher and nearly paid

with his life when a rifle spoke from the blackness along the north wall. He swore he felt the slug brush his ear. Answering in kind, he crawled to a display.

Whoever shot at him from the front corner could not have reached the north wall so quickly. Which meant he was up against two Hinkles, not just one. If he stayed where he was they could catch him in a crossfire. Or they might cover the doorways and wait for the storm to end, then bellow for help from their kin.

Flat on his belly, sticking to the darkest patches, Fargo crawled toward the stairs. At each stab of lightning he froze. He was close to the rail when a shadow separated itself from the corner. He could not quite tell where the head and chest were so he didn't shoot.

Then a revolver cracked and the floor under his chin exploded in shards. He replied in kind and missed. The shadow was on the move toward the north wall, and the other Hinkle opened up to cover him, firing at Fargo's muzzle flash.

Lunging, Fargo seized hold of the rail and pulled himself up and over. The moment his boots smacked the stairs he was in motion. Slugs chipped the wall in front and behind but somehow he made it to the second floor in one piece and flung himself to the floor. The firing stopped and he reloaded.

"We know you're up there mister," bellowed a voice out of the darkness. It sounded like Chad.

"That's right," said someone else. "And we'll keep you pinned up there until help comes."

They were moving as they talked and Fargo could not pinpoint their exact positions.

"Cat got your tongue?" Chad taunted.

"Or is it you're just yellow?" said the other.

Fargo did not waste lead on them. They would be there when he came back down. To reach the roof, he had to go halfway down the hall to a rope that dangled from the ceiling. One tug lowered a folding ladder. At the top was a door. Opening it, he stepped out into the raging elements.

The Colt repeating rifle was in the corner where he had left it. Sheets of driving rain veiled the street and buildings. And if he couldn't see the Hinkles, they couldn't see him. For the time being he was safe.

The storm also hid the house with the stone fence. Fargo had not heard shots from that direction, and he could only hope Devy and Gwen had done as he told them and sought haven in the attic. He went to the door to the roof to be ready in the case the pair downstairs had followed him, but the minutes passed uneventfully.

The inaction took a toll. Fargo had not quite realized how tired he was. Or how sore. He was skinned and scraped and bleeding in spots. His left cheek had been cut by a flying sliver and he had jammed a finger so severely, the knuckle was throbbing. But he was alive, and when all was said and done, nothing else counted.

Raising his face to the storm, Fargo grinned. He owed himself a week in Denver to recuperate. A week of gambling and drinking and doves in tight dresses would have him feeling like his old self in no time. When a man loved life as much as he did, the act of living was its own tonic.

The next moment, as abruptly as it began, the thunderstorm ended. The rain stopped falling and the lightning stopped flashing and the shrieking wind dwindled to gusts, all within the span of seconds.

Fargo couldn't quite believe it was over. The clouds were as dark and ominous as ever. A sound in the street lured him to the edge of the roof. Where before the street had been hard-packed dirt, now it was a lake of mud from boardwalk to boardwalk. Pools and puddles were everywhere. And sloshing down the center were two hellhounds.

With them was Eli Hinkle, his head bandaged. "Pa?" he called out. "Pa, where did you get to?"

"He's not up here," Fargo said, and when Eli glanced up, he shot him between the eyes. The hellhounds leaped for cover but one slipped and slid as if it were on ice and bowled over the other. Fargo had all the time he needed to take deliberate aim. He thought it would bring the two Hinkles below outside but they weren't as foolish as Eli had been.

Fargo scoured the buildings on the other side of the street. He looked toward the church, toward the hills. No sign of more Hinkles anywhere. He started to turn to the south and inadvertently saved his own life. A rifle boomed, the shot louder than a Spencer, louder than the Colt repeating rifle, louder than the Henry, too. It had to be Leon Hinkle's Sharps, and he hadn't missed by much.

Crouching, Fargo spotted him almost instantly. Leon was in the house with the stone fence, at a second-floor window, and had lowered the Sharps to insert another cartridge. Fargo snapped off an answering shot and the window above Leon's head shattered. Leon ducked out of sight.

In a burst of speed Fargo reached the south wall. He aimed at the spot where Leon had been, hoping the patriarch would stand back up, but Leon didn't reappear. Seconds later he heard that which he dreaded most; a piercing scream. It was too high-pitched to be Devona; it must be Gwen. It was followed by a muffled shot.

Fargo ran to the door and raced down the ladder to the stairs. In his haste and his worry he nearly made a fatal mistake. He had taken a long bound when the railing exploded from the impact of a slug. The shot came from across the room. He emptied the Colt revolving-rifle, leaped over the rail, and landed hard on the balls of his feet. To his left was a pile of sacks full of grain. He scooted behind them and sank to his knees to reload the Colt rifle.

In through the front doorway sprang a snarling hellhound. Fargo spun, drew his revolver, and cored its cranium. He didn't take aim. He fired from the hip, as he had practiced doing countless times. But in turning, he exposed his head and shoulders, and whoever was by the north wall promptly fired. The slug struck one of the grain bags and burst through the other side.

Fargo bent to finish reloading the rifle but a new sound intruded. The sound of a horse whinnying in distress. And it was not just any horse, it was the Ovaro. The Colt revolving rifle was suddenly forgotten. So was the concealed assassin across the room. He was out the door before another shot rang out, and sprinted toward the house. He would be damned if he would let Leon Hinkle get his grubby hands on the Ovaro a second time.

Up the street a pistol cracked. Twisting, Fargo returned lead for lead, and someone in the barbershop doorway sprang back. He came to the end of the boardwalk and was confronted by a sea of mud between the feed and grain store and the stone fence. To try to cross it would be suicide. Now that the storm was over, the sky was brightening, and he would be as easy to pick off as a duck from a blind.

"Damn!" Fargo fumed. He was torn between his worry about the Ovaro and the Carroways and a natural urge to preserve his skin. Neither impulse was strong enough to vanquish the other. He hesitated, and heard another whinny from the horse that had saved his bacon more times than there were stars in the night sky. His skin be hanged.

He stepped off the boardwalk and promptly regretted it when his right boot slid out from under him and he was dumped on his back. A shot rang out at the exact same instant and someone bawled, "I got him! I made coyote bait of that mangy buzzard!"

Fargo played possum. His Colt was in his right hand, and he had fallen in such a way that he could see the boardwalks and much of the street. The Hinkles were bound to verify he was dead, and would walk right into his sights.

A figure stepped from the barbershop. "Did anyone hear me? Is anyone else still alive? I killed him!"

Arvil Hinkle walked out of the feed and grain. "I

hear you just fine, Horace. Get up here and we'll take a look-see."

No one else appeared. Nor did any hellhounds.

Without moving his head, Fargo glanced at the Colt and slowly cocked it. Once they were close enough he would send them to join their brothers. His right hand was spattered with mud but he had a firm grip on the six-gun.

Arvil beckoned to Horace. "Hurry it up. I heard some shots from that house yonder. Pa might need us."

Fargo shifted his right arm and inwardly grinned. They were making it easy. Then he saw the Colt's barrel. It was jammed with mud.

12

Jammed firearms could maim or kill. Skye Fargo once saw a man lose part of his hand when he fired a revolver jammed with snow. Another time, a buffalo hunter's Sharps blew up in his face when dirt got into the barrel. The hunter was blinded in one eye and his face horribly scarred.

When Fargo slipped and fell, the Colt's barrel had dug into the mud. He couldn't tell how much was in the barrel but it didn't take much. He had to clear it. But to do that he needed a stick or a ramrod and he had neither.

Arvil was watching him closely, his dark eyes narrowed in suspicion. Horace was still too far away to pose much of a threat.

Girding himself, Fargo rolled to his right. Arvil's rifle boomed and a slug smacked into the mud near his head. Before Arvil could fire again, Fargo was running along the feed and grain to the rear. He was almost there when Arvil's rifle blasted again and the wall at his elbow thunked. He made it around the rear corner but he didn't stop.

The nearest place Fargo could think of that might have something he could use was the general store. He tried not to think of what might be happening to Devona and Gwen. But he had to clear the mud from the Colt. He wouldn't be any use to them dead.

As he passed the gap between the feed and grain and the neighboring building, he glimpsed Horace

Hinkle at the street end, taking aim. A shot cracked but he went past so fast, Horace missed.

Fargo was surprised at the absence of hellhounds. Maybe he had killed them all, although it might be those still alive had taken to the hills. He came to the general store, threw open the back door, and ran down the hall past the hybrids he had slain a short while ago. At the counter he paused. There were so many shelves, so much merchandise. His gaze fastened on a pipe display, and he smiled. Beside it were pipe cleaners. He selected one, and inserted it into the Colt's muzzle. When he pulled it out, it was coated with mud. He inserted a second, a third, a fourth. Only a little mud was on it. He inserted a fifth and swirled it around.

A sound from out front told him he was out of time. Horace Hinkle was in the doorway. Horace spotted him at the same instant.

Hoping to hell the barrel was clean, Fargo snapped up his arm and fired. Horace was punched onto his boot heels, tottered off the boardwalk, and fell spread-eagle in the mud.

Fargo dashed to the doorway and peered toward the feed and grain. Arvil wasn't there. A premonition caused him to turn, and there, at the back door to the general store, was Arvil, about to shoot. He dived for the boardwalk as the rifle went off. Once again lady luck was on his side. The slug whistled over him, and he was up and running, angling across the street to a water trough.

Hurtling it, Fargo dropped to his hands and knees. He could see the house with the stone fence. It was quiet now, with no sign of activity. He wanted to race there and find out if Devy and Gwen were all right, but he couldn't yet.

The wind rustled, blowing strong enough to ripple the water in the puddles.

Fargo was too savvy to look over the top of the trough. Arvil might spot him, and a bullet would go right through it. He had seen men die that way. So he crouched as still as a marble statue until he heard someone swear. He glanced at the barbershop window and in it saw a reflection of the general store, and Arvil Hinkle on one knee beside Horace, a hand on Horace's chest, overcome by grief.

Fargo waited for Arvil to stand so he would have a better target. He was still waiting when a low growl close behind him snapped his head around. He had been wrong about the hellhounds. Crouched low ten feet away was a mud-spattered beast about to spring, its fangs glistening with saliva. Twisting, he fired as it leaped. His shot smashed it in the chest and it fell but immediately regained its feet and charged. He put his second shot into its forehead but it was still able to rise onto its forelegs and snap at him. It needed a third shot. Any moment, he expected a slug in the back.

Instead, he heard the slosh of boots smacking mud.

Fargo whirled. Arvil Hinkle, angrily working the lever of a Spencer, was almost on top of him. The rifle had jammed. That was why Arvil hadn't shot him. Fargo pointed the Colt but Arvil swung the Spencer like a club. Pain spiked Fargo's wrist and his Colt sailed from his fingers. He heaved to his feet a heartbeat before Arvil slammed into him.

They sprawled onto the boardwalk with Fargo on his back and Arvil with the Spencer pressed to his throat, trying to choke off his breath. Fargo bucked and pushed but Arvil was determined. A knee grazed Fargo's groin and the world spun dizzily. He could feel the rifle gouging into his windpipe and knew if he did not do something and do it right away, he would die.

Fargo drove his own knee up and in. Arvil grunted and his grip slackened. Instantly Fargo heaved, flipping Arvil off. Arvil swung a fist at his chin but he absorbed the blow with his shoulder and delivered an uppercut to Arvil's jaw. Ordinarily that was enough to stun most, but he was on his back and had no leverage. All it did was rock Arvil a little. They pushed to their feet. As Fargo rose, he slid his right hand inside his boot. When he straightened, he had the Arkansas Toothpick low against his leg where Arvil couldn't see it.

"Die, damn you!" Arvil raged, and swung the rifle high, trying to cave in Fargo's head.

Dodging, Fargo speared the Toothpick into Arvil's unprotected ribs. It buried itself to the hilt. He yanked the blade out to stab again but it wasn't necessary.

Arvil had gone stiff and was looking down at himself in amazed disbelief. "No!" he bleated, and staggered against a hitch rail. Letting go of the Spencer, he clung to the rail. "You've done killed me."

Fargo kicked the Spencer out of reach and found his Colt. Mud caked the cylinder and the butt but the barrel was clear. He wiped the Toothpick clean of blood and slid it into its sheath.

"You've killed me," Arvil repeated. He oozed lower until he was sitting with his back to the post. Blood flowed copiously from the wound and a trickle appeared at a corner of his mouth. "You've done wiped out nearly all of us."

"How many people have you and your family killed?" Fargo flipped open the Colt's loading gate to reload.

"I don't want to die," Arvil said. Arvil coughed and blood dribbled over his chin.

"Go to hell." Fargo headed for the house, watching the porch and the windows, but he did not see anyone. He ran to the stone fence and circled to the back. The door was open and fresh footprints and hoofprints pockmarked the mud. Placing a hand on top of the fence, he vaulted over. The tracks showed where one man had been leading the Ovaro, another walking beside it. Leon Hinkle and one of his sons.

Where were Devy and Gwen? was the question uppermost on Fargo's mind. It could be they were on the Ovaro but he had to be sure. He hurried inside. Total quiet reigned.

The small door to the attic hung open and the ladder had been left in place. "Devona?" Fargo poked his head into the attic but they weren't there. He wasted no time in rushing back down and out the front door to the gate.

The tracks led south toward the main trail. He figured they had a five to ten minute head start, no more. Shoving the Colt into his holster, he settled into a mile-eating dogtrot. Or tried to. Mud clung to him with every step he took, and after fifty yards, great gobs weighted his legs down like boulders. Again and again he had to stop to scrape off his boots.

By now the storm had drifted to the east and the sky in the west was beginning to clear. The wind was brisk and cool. Only once did Fargo look back, and by then Carn resembled a small row of stacked dominoes.

The afternoon waned. Fargo continued slogging south until he came to the woods bordering the road. By then he was only a few minutes behind the Hinkles and their captives. He stopped for what had to be the hundredth time to clean his boots, only this time he used a broken branch. As he was tossing it aside, he caught the glint of sunlight off metal high in a patch of trees a quarter of a mile ahead. He stared at the trees a while but did not see anything to account for it.

Fargo's legs ached and his finger was still throbbing and his right ankle had been chafed raw but he gave no thought to resting. He went around several bends and spotted the abandoned farm wagon up ahead. The tracks led straight past. He was staring at them as he went by, and that proved to be a mistake.

"This is as far as you go, mister."

The *click* of a gun hammer convinced Fargo not to make a stab for his Colt. Halting, he held his arms out from his sides. "Damn."

"You can turn around if you want. Just don't try anything." Tyrel was on his knees in the wagon bed, and he had Fargo's Henry.

"Where are the woman and the girl?"

"With my pa. He knew you were doggin' us. Don't ask me how but he did." Tyrel made no attempt to climb down. "He sent me up a tree for a look-see, and sure enough, there you were. So he had me wait. Pretty clever of him, wouldn't you say?"

"Have they been harmed?"

"Is that all you care about?" Tyrel shook his head. "Pa hasn't laid a hand on them yet."

"Yet," Fargo stressed. "But we both know he'll force himself on Devona Carroway once he thinks it's safe. Is that what you want?"

"Don't try to turn me against my pa." Tyrel stood and climbed onto the seat. "I should gun you where you stand. If not for his sake, then for all my kin you've rubbed out."

"They were trying to kill me," Fargo reminded him. He was debating whether he could throw himself to one side and draw before Tyrel got off a shot and decided he couldn't. "I'm surprised you haven't shot me yourself."

"I should have. That's what Pa wanted me to do. To splatter your brains all over creation and back again, as he put it. He'll be listenin' for the shot up yonder."

"Why haven't you?" Fargo bluntly demanded, and when Tyrel frowned, he said, "I'll tell you why. Because you don't want anything to happen to Devona and her daughter any more than I do."

"Reckon you have me all figured out, do you?"

"I know you're not like your brothers. They bought your father's lie about your mother having rabies. But we know better. We know he murdered her and we know why."

"I have my doubts, sure, but I can't prove anything," Tyrel replied without conviction. "If I could it would be a different story. I loved Ma dearly."

"What if I could help you prove it?"

Tyrel's finger curled around the Henry's trigger. "You're tryin' to save your skin by trickin' me but it won't work. I have to shoot you whether I want to or not." He paused. "How could you prove it, anyhow? Pa's not about to come right out and admit a thing like that."

"Not to you," Fargo said. "But to me he might if I play my cards right."

"I couldn't," Tyrel said, again without conviction.

"Don't you want to be sure? Don't you owe your mother that much?" Fargo could read the younger man's turmoil on his face. "Or do you want your father to spend the rest of his life thinking he got away with it?"

"You haven't told me how."

Fargo hadn't given it any thought but he did so now, and when he was done explaining, Tyrel slowly nodded.

"That might work. Pa always has liked to crow about himself. But we'll do it my way or we don't do it at all." Tyrel motioned. "Empty your pistol. Do it nice and slow so I can count the bullets as they drop. One wrong twitch and I'll shoot you like a rabid coon, so help me."

Fargo did exactly as he was told.

"Good. Now put the pistol in your holster and keep your hand away from it until we get there." The Henry never wavered as Tyrel hopped from the wagon. "Walk in front of me. It won't be far."

It wasn't. Leon had stopped two hundred yards further on. He had tied the Ovaro to an oak and was pacing from one side of the rutted track to the other. Devona and Gwen were perched on a log, Gwen nestled in her mother's arms.

Moving quickly to keep from being seen, Fargo entered the trees and worked his way nearer. He was conscious of Tyrel a few steps behind him, and of the Henry centered on his back. Moving from trunk to trunk and bush to bush, he soon heard Gwen sniffle.

"Shut that brat up," Leon Hinkle snapped, "or I'll do it for you." He glanced north and shifted his Sharps from one hand to the other. "Why the hell haven't we heard a shot? My boy should have plugged that son of a bitch by now."

"Maybe Fargo was too quick for him," Devy said.

"Then we'd have heard a shot anyway." Leon

slapped his leg in disgust. "I should have done it myself. Never trust a boy to do a man's job."

Drawing his Colt, Fargo slid through a patch of high weeds until he was within spitting distance of the Ovaro. The stallion saw him but didn't whinny or stomp. When Leon turned to gaze north again, Fargo unfurled and stepped from concealment. "Drop the Sharps," he commanded, thumbing back the Colt's hammer.

Leon Hinkle imitated an oak. "So," he said, and angrily threw the Sharps into the mud at his feet.

Devy and Gwen stood up and started toward Fargo but he waved them back. To Leon he said, "I want to see your face when I do it."

The patriarch turned, the stamp of resignation on his features. "That boy always was worthless. Too soft-hearted, just like his ma."

"Is that another of the reasons you murdered her?" Fargo asked, but Leon didn't take the bait.

"Why couldn't Clyde or Chad been with me? They hardly ever let me down." Leon was speaking more to himself than to Fargo. "I had me some good boys and now they're all gone, thanks to you. You've got more luck than all the riverboat gamblers ever born."

"Don't blame me for your mistakes." Fargo tried to catch sight of Tyrel off in the trees.

"It wasn't me who shot them," Leon said.

"It was you who told them what to do, you they were willing to kill for. And it was you they died for." Fargo moved closer but not so close Leon would notice the Colt's cylinder was empty.

"I'd do it the same if I had it to do all over again," Leon declared. "We had a chance to be rich, mister. To have all the things we always wanted. To live like kings instead of always scrapin' by."

Devy expressed Fargo's own sentiments. "There's more to life than money and land. I pity you, Mr. Hinkle. Truly, I do. You were rich and didn't realize it. There's nothing more precious than a son or daughter, and your greed has cost you all of yours."

"Don't lecture me, woman. Sprouts are like pups. You can always raise a new litter if you need to. I have plenty of good years left. You can give me another seven or eight sons, easy."

Fargo pointed the Colt at Hinkle's head. "You're forgetting something, aren't you?"

"I'm not forgettin' anything. But I dare you to put that six-gun down and settle this man to man."

"Maybe I'll give you the chance," Fargo said. "First there's something I'd like to know. Why *did* you kill your wife?" His life at stake, Fargo saw Leon look at him in annoyance and thought he would get no answer.

"Why do you keep bringin' her up?"

"I just want to know what kind of man can do such a thing."

For a few seconds Hinkle stood there with his lips pinched together. Then he let out a long sigh. "Ever lived with a female for twenty-four years? Ever seen a pretty filly turn into a shriveled shrew? Seen the woman you took for your own grow gray and wrinkled before her time and lose all interest in you and anything that has to do with you?" Leon sighed again, only louder. "I did. Month by month, year by year, I saw Agnes wither like a grape on the vine. All the life went out of her. All the laughter. All the fun."

"And whose fault was that?" Devona demanded.

"I wasn't a bad husband. She always had a roof over her head and she never went hungry. And I didn't hardly beat her but two or three times a year. She could have done a lot worse than marry me."

"Yet you killed her," Fargo prompted. Unless Leon confessed, unless he came right out and told them everything, Tyrel would never believe it.

"I just couldn't take it any longer. Couldn't take her not talkin' to me except when the boys were around. Couldn't take how she looked at me with those sad eyes of hers all the damn time. Couldn't take how she wouldn't have anything to do with me under the bedsheets." Leon bit his lip. "That was the worst. A man has powerful needs. But my Agnes wouldn't do her wifely duty."

Fargo tried once more. "So you went and killed her?"

"So I went and blew her brains out, yes!" Leon snapped. "I told the boys she came down with rabies and had to be put down like a rabid hound. Truth was, Agnes was as healthy as a mule. She'd have out-lived me. Would have put me through hell for another twenty years and I couldn't take that."

"Thank you," Fargo said.

"For what?"

"For digging your own grave."

Out of the woods stepped Tyrel. When he spoke his voice was husky with emotion. "I knew it. I told the others but they wouldn't believe me. They said you'd never stoop that low."

Leon's astonishment was short-lived. Fury contorted his face into a mask of livid hatred directed at Fargo. "You tricked me, you bastard! You did this to save your miserable hide."

Fargo was watching the younger Hinkle. Tyrel had the Henry trained on his father but he hadn't cocked it.

"Ma was the sweetest, kindest lady who ever lived, Pa. She loved all us boys and could never do enough for us. She fed us, she sewed our clothes, she tended us when we were sick. She was always ready to listen when we had a problem." Tears poured from Tyrel's eyes. "She gave you the best years of her life and how did you repay her?" He nearly screamed the next. *"You killed her!"*

"We shoot dogs that outlive their usefulness, don't we?" was Leon's response. "Don't make such a fuss over a trifle."

Tyrel was shaking from head to toe. He raised the Henry but he couldn't hold it steady.

"What are you doing, boy?" Leon asked.

"Fixin' to do to you like you did to Ma." Tyrel should have shot then and there but he took another step, blinking the tears from his eyes, and probably never saw the knife Leon slipped from under his shirt sleeve.

Fargo sprang forward. "Look out!"

Tyrel glanced at him and then glanced down but by then it was too late and the long blade had sliced into his abdomen. He uttered a low "Oh!", and collapsed. Leon grabbed for the Henry but Tyrel had fallen on it.

"You're plumb worthless," Leon said, and slit his own son's throat.

Then Fargo reached them. He slammed into Leon and they both wound up in the mud, Fargo with his hand locked tight on Leon's knife arm and Leon with his thick fingers clamped onto Fargo's throat. Fargo tried to dislodge him but Leon's fingers clamped harder.

"Now it's your turn!" Hinkle hissed. His eyes were wide, the pupils dilated, his nostrils flaring. "Die, damn your bones! Die!"

Rolling on his shoulder, Fargo pushed with all his strength but Leon clung on. For a moment there was enough space between them for Fargo to tuck his knees to his chest, and the next second, with an outward sweep of his legs, he catapulted the elder Hinkle from him.

Fargo barely gained his footing before Leon was on him again, spearing the knife at his neck. Dodging, he grabbed Leon's wrist in both hands and twisted. Leon roared like a gut-shot bear. They grappled furiously, Leon fighting with a strength born of pure rage. Suddenly Leon was on top, pressing the blade toward his throat. The tip was a finger's-width from Fargo's jugular when he wrenched almost hard enough to tear Leon's arm from its socket, and sent the knife flying.

Leon spun. Fargo thought he was running away but Leon went only a few yards and stooped to grab the Sharps.

"No!" Devona cried.

"Yes!" Leon bellowed in triumph.

Staring down the muzzle, Fargo took a couple of long steps back and hiked his arms. "Looks as though you've got the drop on me."

"Damn right I do!" Leon roared. "And now I'm about to fix your hash for all the grief you've caused me." Glowing with malicious glee, he sighted down the barrel. "Any last words before I put windows in your skull?"

"It's too bad you weren't stillborn. It would have spared a lot of people a lot of misery."

"Killin' you will be a pleasure," Leon said.

Fargo was staring at Leon's trigger finger, and when it began to tighten, he threw himself to the left, yelling to the Carroways, "Get down!" He was the only one who had seen the mud clogging the Sharps.

The blast was twice as loud as it should be. Fargo heard Leon shriek and looked up to see a jagged six-inch piece of metal jutting from Leon's ruptured right eye. The rest of the burst barrel was still attached but in twisted strands of smoking metal.

Hinkle was dead before he melted to the ground.

Fargo wearily stood. He turned to Devona and Gwen and suddenly they were in his arms, sobbing with joy. "It's over," he said. They could pick up the pieces of their lives and start over again, which was more than most of the settlers could do.

"Any chance we can talk you into staying a few days?" Devy asked, her eyes twinkling with promise.

"I'd like nothing better," Skye Fargo said.

LOOKING FORWARD!

**The following is the opening
section of the next novel in the exciting
Trailsman series from Signet:**

THE TRAILSMAN #265
Dakota Death Rattle

*Black Hills, Dakota Territory, 1859—
Where the ancient laws of the Manitus demand blood,
and the deadliest disease of all is gold fever.*

Overhead, vultures wheeled like merchants of death against a mother-of-pearl morning sky, warning the bearded, buckskin-clad rider that trouble lurked just beyond the next ridge.

Skye Fargo nudged the riding thong from the hammer of his Colt, easing back on the reins to halt the Ovaro. They had just rounded the shoulder of Ragged Top Mountain, well up toward the summit. Now Fargo's lake-blue eyes enjoyed an excellent view of the pine-covered slopes overlooking Spearfish Canyon, bright with splashes of larkspur, daisies, and other wildflowers. A red-tailed hawk soared on a wind current, and here and there among the darkly forested slopes huge chunks of crystallized gypsum flashed in the sunlight. The air was thinner up here, and Fargo felt slightly lightheaded.

White men called these forested mountains the Black Hills, Sioux called them the Paha Sapa. By any name, Fargo considered them one of the great natural surprises of the American West. They formed a virtual island of timber surrounded by level, barren, treeless plain. It was not as arid here as in the surrounding Dakota Territory, because some of the peaks rose more than a mile high. They arrested rain clouds that otherwise quickly blew over the dry plains. Thus these mountains had become a haven for grizzly bears and other wildlife.

Despite their natural beauty and good hunting, however, Fargo normally avoided the Black Hills like he would the mouth of hell. Those wheeling vultures just ahead of him now were not an uncommon sight here.

These mountains were surrounded by Sioux and Northern Cheyennes—no tribes to mess with. And the Sioux, especially strong just west and south of these disputed mountains, were particularly determined to keep gold-seeking white men out of the Paha Sapa. They considered this unique plains oasis the sacred center of their universe.

Fargo knew the Sioux had no legal claim recognized by white men's courts, just squatters' rights. But they were being challenged in the Platte Valley to the south and were determined to keep these sacred mountains free of whiteskins. Fargo saw their side of the matter, too, and had not planned to intrude.

He had been carefully skirting the Black Hills, on his way north to the Yellowstone country. But two youthful Sioux braves, probably looking to earn their first coup feather, had stolen his horse while he was afoot hunting for game. He had been forced to track them east into the Paha Sapa. He stole the Ovaro back without harming either Indian, and now all Fargo wanted was to put this wondrous but troublesome place behind him. Too many fools had come here looking for gold and found only an early grave.

And once again, apparently, danger lay over the next ridge, threatening to snarl his peaceful plans. Fargo kneed the Ovaro forward, seeking low seams. From long habit he avoided the crests of ridges, knowing the swales behind them were favorite lairs of bushwhackers.

Fargo whiffed the scalp-tingling smell of death even before he spotted any actual trouble. A steady buzzing noise increased as they advanced. Soon, huge blowflies annoyed the Ovaro and kept him snorting and flipping his head.

When the stallion began to resist, stutter-stepping sideways, Fargo reined in. He swung his leg over the cantle and dismounted, landing light as a cat. He was tall and rangy, much of his weather-bronzed face shadowed by the slanted brim of his hat. He slid his Henry from its saddle boot and left the reins dangling, knowing his well-trained Ovaro would not wander. Holding the Henry at a high port, he proceeded down the tree-covered slope on foot, leapfrogging from pine to pine as he advanced.

He glanced through a break in the trees and spotted a little clearing carpeted with bluebonnets. Then he looked closer and also recognized pale human flesh lying among the lush grass and wildflowers. Five—no, six bodies, all men, stripped naked and apparently lifeless. Some were covered in a shifting dark blanket of flies.

Fargo felt that familiar quickening of his senses, but remained calm and focused. Confident but careful—that's how a man endured on the frontier. He studied the surrounding trees for several minutes. Birds of every sort serenaded him from countless limbs—a reassuring sign that men were not hiding close by. Nonetheless, he turned sideways to reduce the target for any hidden marksmen when he started across the little clearing.

A sudden voice, quavering and weak, froze him in place like a hound on point.

"God sakes, don't come no closer, mister! I'm a gone-up case. We . . . we all are. It's mountain fever."

Fargo was still about fifteen feet away from the first body. He spotted one fever-flushed, glassy-eyed face watching him. At the dying man's words, he felt a cold sweat break out on his temples. Of all the killers on the frontier, none was more fearsome than the silent horseman called Pestilence.

The man's chest heaved as he tried to suck air into his fluid-filled lungs.

"Too . . . too late now for medicine," he rasped. "They deliberately kept us from a doc."

"Who did? How'd you fellers end up all alone down here?" Fargo asked.

"Forced . . . forced at gunpoint by strangers," the man gasped out. "We're all prospectors. Had . . . had us a claim west of here in Wyoming. Fever hit our camp. A few days later three hired guns showed up, forced a bunch of us . . . forced us to put on brand . . . brand-spanking-new clothes. Then they herded us into a wagon and hauled us . . . here into the Black Hills. Paid some half-breed to strip the clothes back off us and fold 'em up again."

"What happened to the clothes after that?"

But a coughing spasm interrupted the dying man's narrative. Fargo had never had mountain fever, but he knew it was fatal if not treated in time. He also knew he was susceptible now. But sympathy roiled his guts when the man begged for water. He hurried back to the Ovaro and grabbed his bull's-eye canteen off the saddle horn.

However, it was too late. By the time he returned, the unfortunate sourdough was giving up the ghost.

"Just stay back, mister. I can't swallow nothing anyhow. Don't bother . . . burying us," he managed to rasp out on a final breath. "Touching us will—will only kill you. Them . . . goldang vultures'll take care of . . . the remains."

There was a phlegmy rattle like pebbles caught in a sluice gate as the miner's lungs expelled their long, final breath. Fargo had seen death more often than most men, but it never got any easier to watch. He moved quickly around the clearing, verifying that no one else was alive. These men had suffered terribly, deserted and exposed to the elements, and Fargo felt sympathy and anger warring within him. Nor could he help wondering about those "brand-spanking-new clothes" and just who they were intended to infect.

He couldn't bury the men, warning or not, because he had no shovel. But Fargo would be damned if he let those vultures feast, leaving eyeless, flesh-scoured skulls as the final indignity. He spent the better part of an hour scrambling down to nearby Spearfish Creek, returning with boulders and heaping them over the bodies. It was a humble tomb, perhaps, but the best he could manage.

"God have mercy on their poor souls," he muttered, hat in hand, before he returned to his horse.

Even the lowest sinner didn't deserve to die that hard. Yet clearly someone intended to deliberately spread the disease.

Fargo slid his Henry back into its boot, then stepped into a stirrup and swung aboard. He tugged rein and clucked to the Ovaro, heading back up toward the old supply trail he'd been following above, on easier terrain. He was in the northern tip of the Black Hills and planned to keep Spearfish Creek in sight until he emerged out on the surrounding plains. The sooner the better.

"If I owned Hell and the Black Hills," he muttered to his horse, revising a remark he'd once heard an army officer make about Texas, "I'd rent out the Black Hills and live in Hell."

The rough trail was sandy and rocky, with washouts that had to be laboriously detoured. Fargo was forced to dismount often and lead the Ovaro through dense thickets or across shale-littered slopes. At one point, just as he emerged from a thick, tangled deadfall bristling with thorns, the metallic snick of a rifle hammer being cocked halted him in his tracks.

"Hold it right there, mister. Make any quick moves, I'll put daylight through you."

Two men stepped out from the screening timber on both sides of the trail ahead. Their occupation was immediately obvious from the red clay and dark ore stains splattering their clothing and footgear. The prospector who had just spoken was a thickset man who looked strong as horseradish, with wind-cracked lips and a huge soup-strainer mustache. He wore a pair of the new blue jeans produced by Levi Strauss. But it was his long .54 caliber Jennings rifle that got most of Fargo's attention.

"Getcher right hand away from that belt gun!" the man's companion snapped. He was a younger, thinner version of the man with the Jennings except that he aimed an old cap-and-ball dragoon pistol at Fargo's vitals. "Hollis Blackburn must be gettin' confident now, sending only one hired gun to do his dirty work."

"Lower them widow-makers, boys," Fargo replied calmly. "I never heard of any Hollis Blackburn."

"That won't spend, mister," the prospector with the Jennings growled. "If you *ain't* one of Blackburn's gunslicks, how's come you got this far and you're still alive? Now, you just turn back around and go tell him we don't spit when he says hawk."

Fargo knew, better than most, that the West was harsh. But he also knew that most men meant no harm. These two were scared, not criminal.

"Gunslick?" he repeated. "Look close at my rig. Notice the rear sight ain't filed off my short iron, nor the trigger guard cut away. And my holster ain't tied down low. What kind of 'gunslick' do I amount up to?"

The two men exchanged glances at this logic, doubt easing some of the hostility off their faces.

"Well, don't tell us you aim to roost here?" the older one said. "You ain't got the look of a sourdough."

"And how do we know," chimed in the other, "you ain't riding the owlhoot trail?"

Fargo laughed outright. "Would a sane man on the dodge flee *into* the Black Hills? I'd sooner take my chances with a white starpacker than a Sioux war party. I'm only here because two young bucks relieved me of my horse and I had to steal him back."

"You know, Elijah," the younger man remarked to his companion, "this jay looks more like a mountain man or an army scout than a hired gun-thrower. He don't spend much time in rented rooms, that's for sure."

He thumbed the dragoon pistol back to half cock and lowered it.

"Call me Pow," he told Fargo. "It's bobtail for Powhatan. Powhatan Stone. This here is my big brother Elijah."

Elijah hitched his sagging denims. "Beg pardon for the rough reception, Mister . . . ?"

"Fargo. Skye Fargo."

Recognition glinted in both men's eyes.

"Sure! You're the jasper some call the Trailsman," Elijah said. "Not so long back, there was a shooting scrape twixt you and the Danford gang just east of here in the Badlands. Step forward a piece, Mr. Fargo. There's something you oughta see 'fore you go any farther."

The brothers led him about twenty feet ahead to a spot where the tall pine trees had been cleared for lumber. This opened a clear view of the canyon below and a sprawling, ramshackle mining camp. The timber-denuded slopes below them bristled with tar-papered shacks and clapboard shebangs, tents, and even some crude brush shanties. Some of the better constructed dwellings boasted windows with panes of oiled paper. Fargo spotted a portable windmill for driving drinking water to a common well and pump. The prospectors had diverted creek water with ditches and brush dams to grow foodstuffs around their dwellings.

"Welcome to Busted Hump. Population about one hundred and fifty souls, though that number is dwindling. Don't look like much, mebbe, but that place represented a dream to us once," Elijah said with evident pride. "Oh, nobody's been pulling out any fist-size nuggets. But you can still pan gold right out of the creek gravel. Why, with just a pan and a sluice box, a man can earn a living wage and be his own boss."

"But now?" Pow cut in, his tone bitter. "Now it's just a God-forgotten hellhole."

Fargo had his own contrary notions about the "dream" represented by gold fever. By 1859 most prospectors had deserted California's depleted gold fields for Nevada's rich Comstock Lode. Colorado, and recently Idaho, were also swarming with new prospectors. Far from going out, the fires of America's get-rich-quick fever were burning hotter than ever.

If it happened in California, the editorialists were urging, why not rich gold strikes elsewhere? Soldiers, farmers, clerks, school teachers—everywhere men were deserting their jobs, even their families, lured by the promise of wealth.

"I can tell from your face," Elijah said, "that you think we're fools to be here, what with Sioux Indians in these hills as thick as fleas on a hound."

"You ain't fools," Fargo gainsaid. "Any man has a right to seek his fortune honestly. But for every man who hits a bonanza, a hundred more come up with nothing but the sniffles. Meantime, the Sioux are boiling mad and painted for battle."

The gold rumors had persisted ever since an early Jesuit missionary hinted he had seen evidence of it in the Black Hills. Early trappers swore they met Indians using gold-tipped arrows. A reported strike in 1834 ended in disaster with Sioux killing all the miners. Another party in 1852 found gold but had to flee before taking any out.

"Anyhow," Elijah said, "it ain't the Sioux that's been our worst enemy."

Fargo's eyes were trained to read details, and he could fill in some of what Elijah left unspoken. Down below, among the gullies washed red with eroded soil, he could see dark patches where gunpowder had been burned over fresh graves to discourage predators.

His eyes shifted to a building of notched logs, set off away from the rest of camp. It was new and hastily erected.

"That's a pesthouse, ain't it?" he inquired.

Elijah nodded glumly. "As if we ain't got us enough troubles, mountain fever has just hit our camp. We got sixteen people sick already, some of 'em women and kids. Last I heard, that problem hadn't got no farther east than the Front Range in Colorado."

Fargo's gaze cut to the new blue jeans both brothers wore. "Sometimes problems move—or *get* moved. Have you folks recently had a shipment of goods come in—including new clothing?"

Elijah frowned. "Bout three days ago, matter fact. Why?"

Fargo explained his encounter with the dying Wyoming prospector. Both brothers paled at the news.

"Hollis Blackburn, that son of a whore," Pow swore with quiet anger. "He musta somehow had them infected duds slipped in with the rest of our shipment."

"Who is this Hollis Blackburn?" Fargo asked.

"He's a snake-eyed British bastard who'd swipe the coppers from a dead man's eyes, that's who. Calls himself an 'agent' for the Alliance Mining Company," Elijah supplied. "Which means he's the murdering dirtworker for a gang of foreign and eastern investors who back giant mining operations—the strip-miners, the hardrock blasters, the hydraulic operations that wash entire mountains into gravel heaps."

Fargo nodded. He remembered seeing the Alliance Mining Company's clearly posted signs a few miles back from here: WARNING! TRESPASSERS WILL BE SHOT AT AND IF MISSED WILL BE PROSECUTED!

"He's got a mining engineer's report that says Busted Hump sits smack over a rich gold vein just above the bedrock," Elijah added. "We're small potatoes. It's what's *under* our claims he's after."

He pointed at the surrounding pine slopes. "He keeps a bunch of hard tails on his payroll. They're dug in deeper than ticks on a shaggy buffalo. Doing all they can to starve us out of here. We had some good butcher beef until they somehow slipped poisoned grain to our stock. They've even poisoned the local water holes with strychnine to thin out the game hereabouts. Hell, we're boiling old hides to make soup. We're down to our last salt-meat now and whatever fish we can pull from the creek."

"With plenty of air pudding for dessert," Pow chimed in sarcastically. "And since the only law here in the Dakota Territory is lynch law, ain't one thing we can do about it. Us prospectors got the endurance of a door knob, but we're poor shakes as gunmen."

"Now they've gone and infected our camp with fever," Elijah summed up. "And all we got for a 'doctor' is a quack who sells worthless patent medicines, maybe pulls a tooth now and then. Worse, we can't get through to Shoshone Falls to get a real doc. Blackburn's gun-throwers got all the trails covered, and besides, we've ate our last good horse."

"Shoshone Falls," Fargo repeated. "That a town?"

"Town? Hell, it's a bull-and-bear pit," Elijah assured him. "Due south from here, just past Thunderhead Mountain. But they got a real doctor there and a good mercantile."

"It's a damn long chance," Pow admitted, "but the only one we got. Way we figure, if we don't get some medicine in about three days, a good number of us are done for. We need other supplies, too, need 'em bad. It's only about thirty-five miles to Thunderhead Mountain. But it's a rough piece of landscape, made even rougher by Hollis Blackburn's jobbers. They're watchin' us right now, and they'll know that any rider going south is going for help. They'll make it hot for him."

While he listened to all this, Fargo had whistled the Ovaro forward. He opened a saddle bag and pulled out a slab of salt pork wrapped in cheesecloth, handing it to Elijah.

"Just slice it thin and fry it up good," he told the brothers. "It's mean grub and chews like tree bark. I only eat it when I can't tag fresh game. But it'll help tide your camp until I get back with a doc and some supplies."

"Get back?" Elijah echoed. "*You're* gonna risk that trip for strangers?"

"Once a man tells me his name," Fargo said as he stirruped and swung up onto the hurricane deck, "he ain't a stranger, is he? Besides, 'pears I got the only good horse, and I'd rather ride him than eat him."

"It won't be no stroll through the roses," Pow warned him.

"I'm one to give as good as I get," Fargo assured him as he tugged his pinto around. "You fellows hunker down and keep your powder dry. This fandango's just now getting started, and before it's over things will get mighty lively around here, count on it."

No other series has this much historical action!

THE TRAILSMAN

**Available wherever books are sold, or
to order call: 1-800-788-6262**

SIGNET

Charles G. West
HERO'S STAND

Up in the Montana mountains, Canyon Creek is the
perfect little town for Simon Fry and his men to hole
up for the winter. The folks are friendly enough to
open their homes to eight perfect strangers—and
gullible enough to believe that Fry's gang is a militia
sent to protect them from hostile Indians.

Jim Culver is new in town, but he knows something
isn't right about Simon Fry's "militia." They seem
more interested in intimidating people than helping
them. Anyone who questions them ends up dead
or driven out. Someone has to step forward to
protect the people of Canyon Creek from their
new "protectors."

That someone is Jim Culver. And this sleepy town is
about to wake up with a bang

0-451-20822-6

Available wherever books are sold, or
to order call: 1-800-788-6262